GEORGE BARRY
LOST IN BURHAMPTON

Jesse Basset

GEORGE BARRY

LOST IN BURHAMPTON

The Book Guild Ltd

First published in Great Britain in 2022 by
The Book Guild Ltd
Unit E2 Airfield Business Park,
Harrison Road, Market Harborough,
Leicestershire. LE16 7UL
Tel: 0116 2792299
www.bookguild.co.uk
Email: info@bookguild.co.uk
Twitter: @bookguild

This work is entirely fictitious and bears no resemblance to any persons living or dead.

Typeset in 11pt Minion Pro

Printed and bound in the UK by TJ Books LTD, Padstow, Cornwall

ISBN 978 1915122 537

British Library Cataloguing in Publication Data.
A catalogue record for this book is available from the British Library.

To Tom

WEDNESDAY MARCH 24TH

The Spatchcock Society are at it again with their Make Great Britain Great campaigning. They have made a pledge to narrow their privet pruned minds by trying to ethnically cleanse the village. What this amounts to, is trying to force Abdul Aziz to close The Golden Tandoori and pack his bags. They are trying to mount a legal case that his restaurant is creating non-Anglo-Saxon odours that are polluting the local area. Beyond the vile racism, it is hypocrisy of the highest order. Various Spatchcock members, including Chairman Jeremy Simmonds, visit The Golden Tandoori on a regular basis; mostly for takeaways, so they're not seen to be publicly supporting a minority business. I'm under good information that Mr Simmonds is a big jalfrezi fan. As usual, it looks like I'm on my own, or should I say we are on our own. I have the support of Nancy. I would describe her support as muted. She agrees with my intentions but doesn't want to actively engage with them. She wants retirement to be calm. I say, how can you be calm when the world is going to absolute shit and we are surrounded by wankers?

I've had to seek inspiration from dear old Lenin, or Lenny as I like to call him. In the modern day, I'm sure he would have funked up his name to totally connect with a new generation of semi-political, moderately angry and far from radical young people. To this I will return, on occasion, unannounced, but always fully justified in my views and opinions. The great man would be Lenster or VLaLen and would spend hours coming up with witty and provocative hashtags. Maybe #lensaysno or #lenisinareyou or #canceltheflatwhiteandtaketothestreets. So, yeah, Lenny, how did he start a revolution when he was surrounded by ignorant potato farmers and deluded Tsarists? I feel like my life is mirroring his, albeit planted into a different social milieu. I'm surrounded by ignorant morons, trying to hold me back. I just want to sort out this shit, redistribute the fricking wealth and balance this bloody country out. I'm bumping on a few details, but I blame Nancy for this. If she was properly engaged, I'm sure I could resolve the idea that property is theft with our cosy retirement cottage. Actually, what am I worried about? Lenin had a few quid, didn't he – how else did he undertake a revolution? Anyhow, I need somewhere to pissing live, don't question me, you haters (is that with an s or z?).

THURSDAY MARCH 25TH

Day one of Operation Poppadom. I've bought five plain naan breads from Sainsbury's. I wore my Southend United FC cap and my wraparound sunglasses, so nobody could catch me in the act. On reflection, I don't think it was the best disguise, as, as far as I'm aware, I'm the only Southend fan in Burhampton and adjacent parishes. I may be wrong on this, but unlikely. I can spot an Essex twang at a hundred paces amongst these home counties bellends. Wait, is Essex a home county? If it is, it certainly doesn't associate itself with the Land Rover-driving hordes of Surrey. There are quite a few Land Rovers about in Essex nowadays, but I'm sure they are bought for more meaningful and legitimate working-class reasons. I've thought about reclaiming the Land Rover for the proletariat. It can be the people's car for the now – obviously with a different intent, price bracket and political sub-text than VW and the Nazis. That said, nice idea, Hitler, and VW is still going strong. Back to Operation Poppadom. Right, so I have the five naan breads – this operation doesn't actually involve any poppadoms, but I don't like the sound of Operation Naan. It lacks a sense of purpose, that its crunchy snack-based cousin has in spades. So, I'm going undercover: disguise to be decided on, but thinking of black jumper, jeans and woolly hat. Not sure if it will look too *Ocean's Eleven* or such like. No, I've changed my mind, I'm going for black jeans and a camouflaged jacket. It may be a bit *Guns and Ammo* but is well suited for a nocturnal skirmish in semi-rural terrain. I need to teach these Spatchcock fuckers a bloody lesson, Southend-style. I say, Southend-style, but I feel that I'm blending Lenin, as the foundation, Roger Moore in *Where Eagles Dare*, for artistic expression, and Angela Lansbury in her *Murder She Wrote* pomp, for stealth-like execution. The operation is simple yet effective. I'm going to stuff said naans deep into their respective Spatchcock exhaust pipes. That way I'm not only making a statement against their racist views but firing a shot across their gas-guzzling, climate change-denying bows. Nancy insists on keeping the Astra. I've explained on multiple occasions that she has the blood of every dying species on her hands, but she seems fine with it.

I will embark on Operation Poppadom under dark, somewhere between 2 and 3am. Every last one of the bastards will be asleep by then. I would have to bear in mind that as men of a certain age, my age, they will average two to three wees a night, so there is the outside chance of a Spatchcocker taking a piss as I insert a naan. I will be extra vigilant, keeping an eye out for the momentary lighting of bathrooms. I wonder if Lenny had similar considerations when he was about to kick off the Communist Revolution.

4

FRIDAY MARCH 26TH

I woke up in a sweat. I had a nightmare, where I was being chased down the road by giant naan breads with Jeremy Simmonds' face stretched over their undulating doughy surface. I paid a visit to the kitchen to look at the five real naans, ready and waiting for Operation Poppadom. Seeing their bland surfaces, not bearing any resemblance to any leading Spatchcockers, has settled the nerves. I shall now attempt to get a bit more shut-eye.

It hasn't worked. As soon as my head hit the pillow, a Jeremy Simmonds-faced naan is front and centre in the old brain. Piss off, brain, and all your annoying tricks. I take solace that Lenny was an insomniac. I'm fortified by the fact that I've already outlived Vladimir by eighteen years. He may have been able to get more support for his ideas, but my longevity speaks for itself. In Darwin's eyes, I'm the winner. Sorry, Lenny, don't mean to rub it in.

I spent the morning working out my Operation Poppadom route. It starts a mere three doors down, at Chinny Wilkinson's. I've been led to believe that my long-faced, loafer-wearing neighbour was once Permanent Secretary at the Department for Transport. The Permanent Dickhead of the Department of Cocks more like. He's going to get a taste of his own medicine when I shove a hefty Asian bread up his Porsche's downpipe. He didn't have me to deal with when he was leading the charge to deregulate and decimate the public transport system, did he? After seeing to Chinny, I will traverse the village picking off each Spatchcocker until I end with the big one, Jeremy Simmonds. His misanthropy only matched by his prejudice. A private man, who likes to stay out of the line of fire and pull the strings from behind closed doors. I will pierce your defences, Simmonds, and inflict mortal damage on you, your people and your cause, through the deft application of Indian flatbreads.

I had a satisfactory lunch of ham sandwiches, prepared by Nancy. It seems ironic that the quality of the cuisine she serves up has declined in inverse proportion to the time she spends watching cookery shows. I reckon she thinks if she spends time looking at nice food, she doesn't need to bother making it. I sometimes step into the fray of the kitchen and knock up a superb shepherd's pie, in a subtle bid to get her to up her culinary game. I have explained to her that my commitment to creating a grassroots political movement negates my involvement in many household duties. Nancy is unsympathetic. I'm sure Lenny didn't have to take the rubbish out, but anyway, great achievements are built on necessary compromise.

I spent the afternoon walking the Operation Poppadom route with Bobby. As we made our way, I gave him a detailed description of my proposed policy for education. I've called it Piss Off Public Schools and Bible Bashers, or POPSABB for short. It provides the basis for an expedient way of abolishing public and faith schools for the good of the nation. I can tell from Bobby's jaunty manner that he approves. As Nancy spent thirty years as a teacher, I am proposing that she looks at the finer detail. I did raise this with her the other day, but she was preoccupied with watching the preparation of a vegan tagine. I need to catch her at the right moment.

The first three houses offer no major obstacles. Chinny Wilkinson, Rolly Peterson and Mr Cheese all have their cars parked on the front drive, easily accessible from the pavement. It's Spatchcocker four where the problems lie. Terence Swineburne's house is like Fort bloody Knox. There's a ten-foot gate out front and thick hedgerow surrounding his garden. I sent Bobby to investigate. He had a good forage in the Swine's lower hedge area, as we made our way around his pathetic status-signifying boundary: a symbol of wealth and privilege that I will shatter – well, to be more specific, squeeze my way through in the quietest way possible. Bobby's superior reconnaissance skills paid off when he found a small gap of five to ten inches within the hedgerow in the south-east corner of Swineburne's domain. I've put on a bit of weight recently. For this I blame Nancy and her haphazard cooking. With the erratic quality and provision of meals, I've had to increasingly rely on snacks to maintain my stamina for the ceaseless class war. I've tried to explain to her that a revolution can't be based on baked potato, beans and cheese alone. So far, my complaints have not been met. I bent down and crawled into the hedged gap and poked my head through to the other side. Liz Swineburne was weeding her flower beds, but I managed to pop my head back out of the way without being spotted. The gap is too small for my midriff to fit through, so I will have to bring shears and sculpt a hedge tunnel to gain access to the Swine residence. We finished off our walk passing chief Spatchcocker Jeremy Simmonds' house. His Aston Martin was parked up outside his house, in front of his garage. Bobby showed his disdain as we passed by, having a crafty wee on the gravel drive.

I went to bed confident that I can execute Operation Poppadom with the effective precision of senior military personnel or a well-travelled mercenary ninja.

SATURDAY MARCH 27TH

I rose from my bed at 2:00am. The rain was battering against the bedroom windows. Typical. While not ideal conditions, a damp Burhampton is no match for a Siberian winter or a storm in the Urals. Lenny would be unsympathetic. I put on my black jeans and camouflage jacket. I felt a strange energy pulsing through my body. Perhaps this is how my ancestors felt as they prepared for battle. I was glad my battle didn't involve guns and bombs; my war was on a higher plateau. It was a struggle of intellect and ideology.

As I went to the kitchen to retrieve the naans, Bobby started barking. I tried to explain to him that I couldn't combine walkies with Operation Poppadom, but he wasn't having any of it. To cease his barking and avoid waking Nancy, I let him come in tow. I had decided to keep Operation Poppadom a secret from Nancy. She wasn't ready for the hard end of the revolution, or any end for that matter. With the naans in hand and Bobby by my side, I ventured outside.

As we made our way around the route, the rain continued to hammer down. I was unperturbed, but the naans started to get soggy, so I stuffed them safely under my jumper to avoid disintegration. As expected, the first two naans were dispatched into their respective exhaust pipes with aplomb. With confidence rising, I attempted an SAS-style forward roll on Mr Cheese's driveway, as I approached his oversized Mercedes. As I came out of the roll, I felt a twinge in my hip, but it was nothing to worry about. I still have the necessary physical attributes to complete rudimentary gymnastic movements. There's many a millennial who would struggle to match my level of athleticism, but I'll get back to that another time.

With the going good, I readied myself for the Swine's hedge. I took my shears out of my Millets backpack. Green and grey with red trim, this functional yet fetching backpack has been with me through hell and high water. Thanks, Millets. The shears were on the rusty side, and I had to hack for a good five minutes to sculpt a sufficient gap in the hedge. A basic visualisation method involving Monty Don and a steaming mug of hot chocolate allowed me to maintain a sense of equanimity. Perhaps Monty Don would sympathise with my political beliefs and could be co-opted into the role of Agricultural Tsar. I would need to circumvent his glaring privilege through some radical asset stripping. I'm sure he won't mind when his gardens get placed in public ownership. Once the shearing was complete, I crawled through the gap, leaving Bobby behind to keep a watchful eye on streetside activity. I set foot on the Swine's perfectly manicured lawn and had a moment of fear when I spotted that a light was on downstairs. I wiped my rain-splattered glass lenses for a better look but couldn't see any movement. The Swineburnes pay no concern for saving money or the planet. They are just the type of people to leave lights on willy-nilly, as if it doesn't matter. Future generations of Swines will look back and grind their teeth in anger, as they survive on a diet of genetically mutated protein cubes, while dealing with the constant threat of drought, or will it be flooding, or both? Feeling fairly certain no one was up, I made my way around the perimeter of the lawn to the front of the house, my feet squelching on the sodden grass. Once around the side of the house, I swiftly bisected the drive, wedging a naan up the Swine's Land Rover en route to the adjoining road, where Bobby was ready and waiting. He'd cunningly tracked the sound of my feet like some sort of special ops dog. What would I do without you, my little friend?

With Operation Poppadom almost complete, we arrived at Chez Simmonds. I scanned the gravel drive, but the Aston Martin had been removed for safe-keeping into the garage, leaving Jemima's Mini Clubman to the elements. Jeremy Simmonds, you selfish, sexist bastard; you could have let your wife use the garage but no, you are far too important for that. No doubt Jemima, worn down from years of marriage, couldn't care less where he bloody well stuck his Aston Martin. As far as she was concerned, he could reverse it up his arse. Poor woman.

Here was my dilemma: do I punish the oppressed wife of the enemy or walk away leaving the chief Spatchcocker's residence unscathed? I conferred with Bobby, and we agreed that the Mini Clubman was necessary collateral damage on the road to revolution. We would inflict de facto pain on Jeremy Simmonds and, in turn, still make our point. This was realpolitik at its finest. I hoped Jemima could one day look back and be proud of the important part she had made in the downfall of the system.

Bobby and I trod lightly on the gravel drive to avoid detection. Nearing the Clubman, I went down on all fours and carefully rolled the naan before shoving it into the exhaust. A wave of euphoria washed over me. I think Bobby felt equally jubilant, as he skipped by my side back home. I hadn't felt this good since Southend were promoted to the Championship in 2006.

Arriving home, I poured a cheeky celebratory glass of the old plonk, not forgetting an extra-large portion of treats for dear Bobby. I indulged myself in imagining the reaction of the Spatchcockers as their cars tried to splutter into life. My favoured image was of Chinny Wilkinson, spewing vitriol when encountering the offending flatbread. Oh, what joy. I slipped back into my favourite pyjamas, sneaked into bed and at 3:30 fell into what can only be described as the sleep of champions.

Nancy marched into the bedroom at 9:00, worried that I'd fallen into a coma. The last time I'd slept beyond 8:00 was after a bout of bad jet lag on return from a trip to New York. She shook me awake and quizzed me on my idleness. I put my uncharacteristic lie-in down to old age and shared a conspiratorial smile with Bobby, as I made my way down for a late breakfast. Lenny would have looked down on such tardy behaviour but would have understood, once I'd explained to him the details of my nocturnal cunning.

Nancy went out for a game of mixed doubles at Burhampton Tennis Club, leaving Bobby and me alone. I have lectured her repeatedly that tennis is a sign of bourgeoisie decadence not fitting for the wife of an eminent radical, albeit in his later years, but she won't be drawn into conversation on the issue. The Swineburnes are members, for crying out loud, and she is happy to rub shoulders with them. Next she'll be inviting them over for dinner. I could knock up a chilli con carne and regale them with the tenets of *The Communist Manifesto*, as they gulped their expensive wine down their bigoted necks.

I deliberated whether I should go and walk around the village. My best tactic could be to hide under plain sight. I put off my decision and made my way on to the internet superhighway, heading straight for the Burhampton Forum. I scanned the forum topics and there, nestled between '*Charity Cake Sale*' and the '*Rising Cost of Plums*', was '*Car Bread Attack!! Hooligan Alert!! Watch out!!*', created by Simmonds53 at 8:45. The chief Spatchcocker had barely finished his breakfast before surfing the cyberwaves to vent his spleen. I have them riled, comrades.

I clicked on the topic link and my eyes lit up when I saw the discussion that had unfurled. Simmonds53 had started the ball rolling by describing at length how a hooligan had tampered with his wife's prized Clubman. Within three responses the conspiracy theories started spreading like wildfire.

RevRightOn (Reverend Ormerod) suggested that it may be an ISIS splinter group, on the basis that they, '*like those sorts of breads, don't they?*'

MrCheeze (yes, Mr Cheese) thought it may be Larton Bowls Club, as there was a heated dispute with the

Burhampton 1st Team in their last contest. It had something to do with illegal bowl lubrication, but the finer detail was lost on me.

Swinster (The Swine) piped up, taking umbrage that his Land Rover had been penetrated by a foreign baked good. *'If this was some sort of retaliation from Mr Aziz, then there would be hell to pay.'*

While I felt pleased that no one had even thought that this was the work of a left-wing master of agitprop, I had a pang of guilt for putting Abdul in the firing line. I thought quickly to rectify the situation. I created a false name, Lenny19, and waded in with a swift response. I spelt out how, *'the naans in question were most certainly supermarket-bought and not the sort of fare that a reputable restaurant would proffer.'* My relief was short-lived.

In my haste, I hadn't thought through my comment and Swinster was quick to swoop on my error. *'How do you know what type of naans were used? Was your car also defiled?'*

At this point I panicked and deleted my profile. This triggered several posts about the identity of Lenny19. Fortuitously, the captain of Larton Bowls Club is Len Jones, so the finger of blame was pointing strongly in his direction. At that point, I decided to log off and get out of the digital mire that I had started to sink into.

Nancy returned from tennis later in the morning. She'd bumped into Liz Swineburne, who had relayed what is now being referred to as Naangate. Since this morning's forum discussion, the Spatchcockers had been in cahoots and deduced that they had been singled out. They had concluded that it was a direct attack on their Make Great Britain Great campaign, which ruled out Larton Bowls Club.

Jeremy Simmonds, squigged naan in hand, had confronted Abdul, but echoing my rogue forum post, he said he would never be seen handling an inferior supermarket bread. The Spatchcockers were stumped. They had no idea who would be behind such an attack. Since moving to Burhampton, I'd been keeping my socialist revolutionary cards to my chest in preparation for this day. Maybe it had been noted that I hadn't put up their 'Close the Tandoori' and 'Take control of the smell of Burhampton' posters, but a man could only go so far in his attempts to go undercover.

I decided to wait until nightfall to take Bobby for a walk. I wasn't in the mood to talk Naangate with anyone just yet. I needed time to plan my next step. I had the welcome distraction of a call from Sophie. She and, who she now refers to as her fiancé, Nathan are going to stay next weekend. Sophie has recently adopted a flexitarian diet to limit her impact on the planet. I'm happy that my radical political views are starting to have an influence on her behaviour. I've discussed the possibility of reducing our meat and dairy consumption with Nancy, but she can't rid herself of a dependence on cheap factory-farmed animal produce. If she is going to keep buying bangers, chops, mince, chicken breasts, chocolate, butter, milk and cheese, what can I do but help her eat them? Perhaps Sophie can convince her of the merits of plant-based cuisine, because I certainly can't. I have to admit that life without cake or a proper cuppa would be pretty bleak, but not as bleak as the complete destruction of humanity. It's all about perspective, isn't it?

I'm not sure if Nathan is also a flexitarian. I've only met him a few times. He's a personal trainer, or PT, as he likes

15

to refer to himself. Sophie said when they met they bonded over their mutual love of planking. In my day, we bonded in more traditional ways that involved a few pints on a Friday night and chancing your arm, with the assistance of some carefully selected chat-up lines. Now they have apps for that. It's too depressing for words, so I'll leave it there.

Whenever I've tried to engage Nathan in conversation, he doesn't seem interested. He doesn't follow football and, as far as I can see, has no political opinions. He seems mostly interested in fitness (like sport but with the fun removed), *Sun, Sex, Hook Up or Get Lost* (I'm sure Sophie could do better), cars (yawn) and clothes (I think he counts as a metrosexual. Get a bloody grip, mate). I could use Nathan as a test bed for how to engage the politically disinterested. I just need to make class war seem as inane and superficial as possible, and he might just go for it. In fact, perhaps I could appoint him my Minister of Youth. I could get him to dumb down my thoughts, to help communicate with people of his approximate IQ and love for indoor machine-based cardiovascular monotony.

At 9:25pm I finally plucked up the courage to leave the house with dear Bobby, forever dependable, by my side. We walked quietly in the night, through the outer fringes of the village. Bobby seemed subdued; hardly surprising after last night's high jinks. As we glided through the cold air, I reflected on the momentous events and started plotting my next move. While the naans had ruffled the Spatchcock feathers, I needed to mount a fresh attack with lasting impact. I felt a strong desire to blow my own cover and take the enemy head-on. The only problem is they may do me for criminal damage. For the time being, I would be the Banksy of radical politics. Yes, who needs an identity these days anyhow? The fuckers at Facebook would only use it to spam me with targeted hair-loss adverts. Anonymity is the new fame, comrades. I would be masked like the Lone Ranger, and, yes, Bobby could be my furry little Tonto. We could ride (walk) the plains (roads) and fight injustice across the Wild West (Surrey), while leading the crusade for a better world (overthrowing the political system and, replacing it with a fairer method of distribution of opportunities, wealth and public services – details still to be ironed out).

SUNDAY MARCH 28TH

I started the day thinking about suitable costumes for a masked socialist superhero and his four-legged companion. Under normal circumstances, Nancy would lead on household fashion decisions, but in this situation I need to adopt her eye for style. Nancy left to go on the weekly shop, which seems to happen three or four times a week, but that's for another time. I was free to dive back online without her prying eyes in the vicinity. While she seems oblivious to most things I do nowadays, I don't want to be taking any chances.

I couldn't resist a foray into the Burhampton Forum. The '*Car Bread Attack!! Hooligan Alert!! Watch out!!*' topic had subsided with only one comment in the last twelve hours. It was from RevRightOn, who was still convinced that ISIS were to blame. Wake up, Reverend, and start tending to your pissing flock. Feeling happy that the cyber coast was now clear of imminent danger, I revelled in the freedom of an online image search to look for inspiration for my new alter ego. The simplicity of the Lone Ranger's black mask covering his eyes set against a red neckerchief, fitted the bill perfectly. As for Bobby, I was less sure, as adorning a dog with any items of clothing make them more not less visible. His alter ego would need no change in appearance. Through the wonders of online shopping, I procured a suitable mask from Fancy That Fancy Dress of Newcastle upon Tyne. I punted for a Zorro mask in the end, as it appeared to have a couple of centimetres' more width than the slightly skimpy mask favoured by the Lone Ranger, thus offering a more substantial disguise. It meant a greater investment, as it came with a hat, cape and sword. I briefly entertained incorporating these into my alternate persona but considered it an over-indulgence. The Zorro fancy dress had an average of four stars in customer reviews and had proved satisfactory for a range of men from the North East. Perhaps the sultry allure of Zorro had a particular resonance in their damp and dreary climes. I also selected a red neckerchief and added it to my basket. Click, done, two days estimated delivery: the optimum time I needed to plan, and plan, comrades, I must.

Later in the day, I convinced Bobby that a quiet Sunday afternoon pint was in order at The Fox and Hounds. Nancy had no intention of leaving the house, setting me free for some good old me time. I do spend a lot of time on my own, but mostly engaged in the revolution, where I feel the collective spirit in my soul, nourishing my appetite for change. Yes, it was time to chillax, have a pint and recharge. If Lenny had taken a leaf out of my book, he may have lasted a couple of decades more at the helm. If only I could go back in time, I could release a dose of super-charged mindfulness in his direction. I'm sure he would have been receptive, whereas I doubt Trotsky and Stalin would have paid the slightest bit of interest in the benefits of meditation. It's on these small details that the course of history can pivot.

The pub visit turned out to be quite eventful. Chinny Wilkinson and Rolly Peterson spotted my solitary pint and made a beeline. It seems in village life nobody can leave you be. It's a by-product of the terminal boredom and existential crisis they all inhabit. I was reading through the match reports from Saturday's games in *The Observer*. I kept the front page hidden so as not to signify my left-wing credentials. That said, *The Observer* rarely strays into the domain of challenging critiques of capitalism. The editorial team seem too preoccupied in reviewing overpriced furniture and East London gastro pubs to have time to contemplate the struggles of the common man.

Chinny had attempted to form a friendship in the past, but I'd been successful on seven or eight occasions in repelling his advances. Nancy, on the other hand, accepted an invite to dinner once, which turned out to be what you would categorise as a socially awkward encounter. During dinner he talked, at length, about his passion for British military history. I threw in my pacifist card midway through a soliloquy to the Battle of Waterloo and I was rebuked as a green-at-the-gills, yellow-bellied pinko. What's with all the colour-based political descriptors, Chinny? Think outside the piggin pencil box. With guys like this at the helm of British transport policy for the last thirty years, no wonder the roads are chock-a-block, and the trains never run on time. While the railways were being privatised, he was fixating on a pincer movement by the Rifle Brigade from 1754. His mind is stuck in the dark ages.

Events didn't improve when the main course was served. While I tucked into the tasty beef bourguignon, I had to remind Chinny and his charming yet mildly irritating wife, Davina, that we should all reduce the amount of red meat we consume if we want to be serious about saving the planet. Chinny said that I was talking rot, and that the empire was built on a good bit of British beef. He then had the gall to call me a hypocrite for eating the said beef. I explained that a fruitful life was built on such concessions, and I was happy to play by their environmentally destructive rules while under their roof. Davina quickly changed the conversation to some vacuous celebrity gossip. Nancy is very good in these situations, as she has her finger firmly on the pulse of the banal world of mainstream media. I've tried to steer her away but realise it is a necessary opium to numb her from the troubles of the world. We all have our vices, mine being a love of sixties easy listening music. 'Up, Up and Away' by the Fifth Dimension is my failsafe song for times of trouble. It's amazing how the perfect combination of lush strings and dreamy lyrics, delivered with mellifluous aplomb, take me to a happy place. It doesn't have the urgency to be the anthem for the revolution, but it will most certainly feature on the soundtrack. The change in topic worked well in diffusing the tension by isolating Chinny and me from the conversation. I did contemplate entering back into the discursive fray by giving my critique of the complicity of popular culture in the decline of civic values due to the aspirational dichotomy at the centre of a self-serving screen-based post-industrial existence but thought better of it. I filed it away to be used in front of a more receptive audience.

Since the dinner party, I would describe interactions between myself and Chinny as strained yet civil. So when he approached me in the pub, I was put on the back foot, or, using his terminology, I needed to lead a rear-guard action after an unexpected attack from an enemy sortie. Chinny sat down, gave me a firm slap on the back and referred to me as 'pal'. I have the 7% guest ale to thank for this surprising show of friendship. Rolly sat beside him in silence, nodding at his every word. He was an obedient lapdog to the Spatchcock cause.

Chinny gave me the heads-up on all the village gossip. Allegedly, Mr Cheese was having an affair with Tatiana, his Polish cleaner. It transpired that the Spatchcockers were fine with his dalliances, as long as he checked she had legal status. This was priceless intel. The booze was loosening Chinny's tongue very nicely indeed. I started to relax as my first pint was finished and Rolly Peterson generously bought me another, accompanied by a bowl of wasabi nuts. These Spatchcockers play fast and loose with ethnic cuisine when it suits.

Eating the tangy Japanese snacks, I spluttered as the conversation turned to Naangate. It was if a switch had flicked in Chinny's brain and the chummy repartee was replaced with his more natural state of aggression. He was convinced that there was a rebel in the midst or the mist (it was quite hard to make out exactly which, as he was slurring his words by this point. I don't think men of his age should be indulging in whisky chasers at three in the afternoon).

22

I internalised my anxiety and kept an unflinching poker face as I listened to his concerns. He thinks the rebel element could be a radical environmental group, but he couldn't find out information of any such organisation in the local area. I said I'd keep my eyes out for any suspicious behaviour. Result – they don't have an inkling I could be the mastermind behind the Asian breaded guerrilla activism. They are quite happy to view me as a daydreaming ageing eccentric reactionary. Appearances can be deceptive, my dear friends. Chat turned to village tittle-tattle. I extricated myself when Rolly Peterson suddenly burst into voice and waxed lyrical on the prize parsnips he was nurturing in his attempt to bag first prize in the village fair. I had a small pang of guilt as I left the pub, as Rolly was the type of man who was serially ignored, but I couldn't bear being in the company of Chinny a minute longer.

I batted the guilt away, feeling energised that I was operating under their noses without raising the slightest suspicion. I had condensed and applied the learnings of *The Art of War* (which I regret to say I haven't read) by keeping my friends close but my enemies closer. It would be hard for Bobby to understand this new hierarchy of interpersonal closeness, but if the time arises, I will teach him some of the lessons of Asian military strategy. As I strode home I pictured my masked self, reeking holistic methods of socialist vengeance on hedge fund managers and ex-media executives alike. If Edward Woodward could equalise the injustice on the mean streets of America, then I could do the same in the mean-minded enclaves of Surrey.

MONDAY MARCH 29TH

Nancy was off out of the house again. She insists on volunteering at the local primary school to help children struggling with reading and writing. It's laudable that after thirty years in education, fifteen as a head teacher, she is still fulfilling her civic duty. My fear is that she is too institutionalised to challenge the world that has shaped her. While my career in the Basildon Council Housing Department may not have had the first-hand impact on the next generation, it has given me an in-depth knowledge of the instruments of power, that I'm now free to overcome. OK, the power welded by Basildon Council is limited to the territory of postcodes SS13 to SS16, but I see it as a microcosm of the nation's ills. Corrupt, indolent bigwigs overseeing budget cuts, spending most of their time at so-called 'important meetings' and 'stakeholder workshops'. Some have the audacity to masquerade as having a social conscience, as they hand another planning contract to an unscrupulous property developer whose idea of 'affordable housing' would only cut the mustard with city commuters. Those brainwashed zombies enduring their subjugation to the capitalist overlords of doom and destruction.

While Nancy is out providing a valued service, while helping prop up the diseased status quo, it is left to true believers in radical thought and transformation, like me, to make a real difference. We, the radicals, have put up with things for too long. We've stayed quiet, ignored and left at the fringes. Well, our time has come. I looked at Bobby and he gave me a reassuring nod. I just can't take it anymore: it's time for action. Well, let's be realistic, the action can wait one more day until my Zorro mask turns up. Without my mask, I have no strength. I lie exposed to the evil powers that look to undermine me. That being the case, a relaxing walk with Bobby in the local woods, followed by a nice nap, are just what is needed on the eve of the awakening of my new persona. I have decided on Fairness Man as a suitable sobriquet. It communicates my raison d'être, with a sprinkling of verve and dash of valour. Like the superheroes of yore, he will smite the villainous forces, in the shape of the Spatchcock, and lead us to better days.

Nancy returned from her day at school and woke me from my hugely enjoyable afternoon slumber. In my next life, I hope to be Italian. That said, if I'd been born into the laissez-faire bonhomie of the Mediterranean, I doubt I would make the same lasting impact on the world. With the daily distractions of coffee, gelato, pasta and a drip feed of ham and cheese, I doubt I'd have the stomach for the complete overhaul of a corrupt political system built on bribes, lethargy and misogyny.

Nancy was full of vigour after her day dipping her toes back into the educational waters. Now I have a secret persona, albeit a work in progress, I need to build a firm wall between my covert activity and daily home life. I will still enter into political discussion but draw the line at divulging any of my emerging strategies. As far as Nancy is concerned, life would carry on as normal, oblivious to the historically significant events that were unravelling under her own roof. As for strategies, I must spend time on my short-term action plan. I earmarked tomorrow morning for a brainstorming session in the conservatory with Bobby. God (the atheist version of God which is essentially nobody), I'm so active, I'm channelling Lenny at full tilt. It was this sort of dynamism that maintained my index-linked salary for over two decades.

TUESDAY MARCH 30TH

The day started with a frisson of excitement as the doorbell rang. I walked swiftly and efficiently to the door, intercepting Nancy en route. There, dressed in navy blue slacks, polo shirt and baseball cap, was an honourable delivery man, box in one hand, digital device awaiting a signature in the other. Nancy enquired about the contents of the box, but I brushed this off by saying, 'Nothing to see here,' combined with a cheeky wink. As it's her birthday next month, she probably thought it was a gift chosen with love and care. The coast was clear, or so I thought. Like an excitable child on Christmas Day, I bounded up the stairs to our bedroom to unveil the goods that lay beneath the cardboard exterior. Laying the box on the bed, I removed the tape that ran through its centre. There within a further unnecessary layer of plastic, was the Zorro fancy-dress outfit with additional red neckerchief. I placed the plastic rapier sword to one side. Its cheap factory-produced finish hadn't captured one ounce of Zorro's noble heritage, thus ratifying my decision not to include it as part of my disguise. The mask and cape were made of a stylish cotton polyester blend, which I was extremely happy with. I made an about-turn based on my gut instinct; I would add the cape to my pallet of visual deception. The neckerchief's bright red, this time 100% cotton no less, was simply captivating. It would provide that dash of colour and socialist semiotics that my followers craved (or will crave once they see it).

It was time to adorn my new garb. Raising the mask up in line with my eyes, I realised I'd overlooked a major technical consideration: glasses. Fairness Man would most certainly need to be able to see. Thankfully, the mask had sufficient length and girth to span my specs. It gave the mask an unconventional but striking look. I put on the cape and neckerchief and took several deep mind-cleansing breaths in preparation for looking at the mirror. I turned and had what can only be described as an out-of-body experience. It was as if a different person was looking back at me. Someone with greater powers than I could ever imagine. From a £14 investment, I had been reborn as an invincible force for the greater good. Having the responsibility of holding such power does feel overwhelming, but I can cope with it. Twenty-two years and three months of dealing with the internal politics of Basildon Council has built an unwavering shield of resilience that is hard to puncture.

What I wasn't to know, was that my new-found invincibility was about to be tested from the off. The adrenaline pumping through my veins clouded my judgement and I decided that I should see what the cape would look like in action. Fair enough, I hear you cry, but not so clever on acoustically resonate laminate floorboards. As I broke into a canter back and forth across the room, cape flowing, mind racing with the possibility of adventure, little did I know that my bounding feet resounded throughout the ground floor, whilst Nancy was in discussion with Burhampton Environmental Trust, in her bid to volunteer on a project to conserve the local woodland. Nancy's altruistic nature has no bounds, even if she should be looking at the bigger picture of climate change and mass extinction, rather than tending to the local shrubbery. I do wish she would broaden her horizons, but she is quite happy to remain steadfast within her comfort zone. The incessant noise of my stomping feet was too much for Nancy to bear. Mea culpa, comrades, in the heat of the moment I had overlooked the auditory annoyance I was reeking throughout Barry Towers. Without warning, Nancy stomped up the stairs and flung open the bedroom door. There I was, in broad daylight, dressed as Fairness Man. Nancy was used to my harmless yet eccentric foibles, but my new identity threw her somewhat. After an initial bout of hysterical laughter, she seemed to be able to contain her obvious glee and ask what I was up to. I thought quick on my feet and said that I was going to audition for a part in an upcoming local amdram production. This took her by surprise, as I have never shown the slightest interest in treading the boards. In fact, I had normally belittled the pompous luvvies, preening themselves in the pretence they provided some sort of worth to civilisation beyond an entertaining anaesthetic that helps shroud the super-rich, supressing the truth behind their evil plots to control society. I explained away this dramatic ethical U-turn as the result of a creative epiphany, where I was met by a vision of Jeremy Irons who proclaimed me as the rightful heir to the thespian crown worn by Larry Olivier, who, from the grave, had been fending off the grubby hands of Benedict Cumberbatch, as they stretched up towards his revered theatrical head. If I can ensure the crown bypasses Cumberbatch's inflated bonce, then I'm happy to oblige. Then one thing led to another and before you know it, I'm practising a five-minute monologue in the character of Dick Turpin, in the outside chance of getting a part in *Murder on the Orient Express*. I informed Nancy that I was happy with whatever part they gave me but had my heart set on giving my unique take on Poirot. Admittedly, my French accent is a bit rough around the edges, but by curtains up I'd be putting Suchet in the shade, where, let's face it, he deserves to lurk amongst the other ITV4 televisual detritus. To say Nancy was dumbstruck was an understatement. She retreated to the ground floor, and nothing more was mentioned on the matter for the remainder of the morning.

Packing the costume safely away in my sock drawer, I headed to the conservatory for the brainstorm session. I called Bobby in to join me, but he immediately lay down for a snooze in his basket. He was signalling to me that I, as the master, was in charge of idea generation. An example of primal behaviour at its finest. Let's face it, dogs have not yet evolved to think 'blue sky'. It just isn't, and hopefully never will be, in their nature. They are devoted servants, and long may that continue. Free to lead the cognitive charge, I opened a fresh notebook and, with a reassuringly sharpened pencil, got the Barry mental cogs turning.

With a visit imminent from an environmental officer to check on potential air infringements from The Golden Tandoori, I turned my attention to pastures new and two topics close to my heart: corporate greed and gentrification. While I like a nice latte and an almond croissant as much as the next man, woman or genderfluid individual, the opening of a soulless American coffee shop, whose name will not pass my lips, replacing the local greasy spoon cafe, is a stretch too far. I can't remember the name of the cafe and had never set foot inside it, but where is the working man, woman or genderfluid individual supposed to go nowadays? Word on the Burhampton streets is positive. Coffee shops are deemed a good addition that can only help inflate (the already astronomical) house prices.

What I'm proposing is a caffeine tax in a bid to both hit the corporates and the wealthy where it hurts, while simultaneously redistributing wealth. It would be a clever hybrid of corporation tax and a progressive income tax system based on customer income and assets. While it may create a degree of pricing complexity for any premises selling hot caffeinated drinks, its ends justify its means. I need someone comfortable with economics to help me flesh this one out, as complex tax policy is not my bread and butter. In the interim, I need to make an immediate impact that will send ripples across the land. Sort of a meta-butterfly effect, if you know what I mean. I think of my black mask and cape, and all becomes clear; I will become the Robin Hood of hot beverages. I will swipe cappuccinos from the hands of the rich and give to the poor. Admittedly, Burhampton doesn't have many people who you would describe as poor, but Larton, approximately 2.25 miles to the north-east, has a growing underclass of pensioners who can't afford a second home in France. By this yardstick, Nancy's and my humble existence could be classified as economically deprived, but this is only fitting of my views and values. By virtue of not owning a gîte in Provence, I am living the suffering of the blighted masses. My anger is real, comrades. Pen in hand, I started plotting my hot drink redistribution strategy. I picture Fairness Man cycling (as he is strictly carbon-neutral) with a trailer behind laden with the appropriated drinks of Burhampton. Mask tightly fixed and cape fluttering in the wind, he shall ride into Larton. There he shall identify worthy recipients of his plunder, before disappearing into thin air, leaving people in awe at what they have witnessed. This will rank alongside the Tolpuddle Martyrs and the Peterloo Massacre as a defining milestone in the class struggle.

I flipped open my laptop and checked the going rate for a bike trailer. At £60 upwards, I decided on fashioning my own bespoke solution. While my DIY skills are limited, I felt confident in being able to construct what is essentially a box on wheels. I went into the garage to rifle for potential component parts. In the space not dominated by the Astra, is stored an array of interesting and overlooked items from the Barry archives. The dusty artefacts of our existence, edging towards obsolescence and landfill. The fact that Fairness Man will be reusing elements of this personal detritus, will only add to his kudos. I meticulously sifted through the miscellaneous items and found what I needed – an old-fashioned pram in a functional blue canvas with a white fur lining, held sturdily in place by a steel frame mounted on hard plastic wheels. Many a time I pushed Sophie around the streets of Basildon in this regal infant chariot. I inspected its coffee-carrying potential and deduced that it had the capacity for approximately twenty-five to thirty coffees (regular not large). I wheeled my treasured Raleigh racer around the Astra, so it stood proud by the pram – two sturdy examples of great British engineering uniting in the struggle for equality. The Raleigh, purchased second-hand in 1992, was blue and white, just like the mighty Southend, and had been fitted with a dynamo lighting system. While the dynamo's rubber-based friction created a degree of drag that prevented me from hitting my top speeds while cycling at night, it was something I was happy to endure in my bid for an emission-free existence.

Then thinking laterally, I expanded my search beyond the garage and visited the garden shed, where I obtained a metre length of sturdy bamboo. Using a Phillips screwdriver, I made holes at each end, through which I passed string that I used to tie the bamboo to the pram's steel frame and to the Raleigh's seat post. I felt the need to have a trial run of my newly constructed trailer. I made my way to the kitchen and selected four mugs of lesser quality, in case of accidental damage, and filled them with water. Nancy looked over and gave me a quizzical look, but I could tell she was holding back on asking me what I was doing. After the earlier mask incident, I think she is leaving me to my own devices. I carefully placed the mugs within the covered area of the trailer where my darling daughter's body would have once lain warm and protected from the bitter winds of eighties Essex. I opened the garage door, mounted my Raleigh and cycled down the drive and onto the road. With only four mugs to weigh it down, the trailer had a degree of lateral movement, which meant that the mugs bounced from side to side, toppling them within seconds. This was a major issue. If I couldn't transport coffee cups without retaining any liquid, my scheme would be a disaster. Luckily, I had some small red plastic-coated bar bells, which I had purchased on a whim from Argos but never used. As I leafed through the laminated catalogue, small biro in hand, their compact shape and reasonably priced answer to a more toned upper body had caught my unsuspecting eye. Since this misguided purchase, I have come to terms with the fact that I'm not designed for weight-lifting. The heavy lifting I do is mental, not physical, and I'm pleased for that to be the case.

I placed the bar bells in the trailer and went for another jaunt down the road with a new batch of tap water filling the four mugs. After two minutes' cycling, there was approximately 35–45% loss of water from the mugs. I had a further brainwave. I'd decant the requisitioned coffee into takeaway cups, before placing spill-proof lids on top. I know, I know, I'm adding to the sea of non-recyclable bile spewed out daily, but I can't tackle everything in one fell swoop. I would then provide further support and shock absorption by surrounding the cups with towels: soft, freshly laundered and ready to play their small yet vital role. The elements of my coffee-transporting system were a fitting metaphor for the layers of thought and involvement that would coalesce into a proletarian powerhouse for radical change.

WEDNESDAY MARCH 31ST

I was feeling excited and anxious. Today was the day that Fairness Man would be unleashed on the world. Having never had a dual persona before, I had no idea what it would feel like once it was 'public'. Despite my undoubted intellect, I had kept a low profile most of my life. I had been happy to be the wind that inflated others' sails. During my tenure in Basildon Housing Department, I had revolutionised the filing of tenant complaints using a combination of dates, names and postcodes. In its specialist area of municipal housing, it will come to be seen in a similar ingenious light as the Dewey Decimal is to librarians. John Moffat, the Head of Basildon Housing Department, directed most of the credit for my filing system in his direction. The selfish egomaniac built his career off the back of the brains and hard work of others. When he lies alone on his death bed, loved ones nowhere to be seen, I hope he regrets his vile ambition. Like most true geniuses, I'm unlikely to get the credit I deserve. I'm happy to be selfless in the relentless pursuit of efficient municipal administrative systems.

Thankfully Burhampton Environmental Trust had signed Nancy up and she was straight off and into the woods to help conserve. What and how she was conserving I had no idea, but I was pleased to be left alone to prepare for Fairness Man's first outing. Entering our bedroom to get changed into my disguise, I placed the theme from *Black Beauty* on the Bluetooth speaker. Its rousing tones filled my chest with pride. Rifling through my wardrobe, I rounded off Fairness Man's look by selecting a plain black sweatshirt and bog standard indigo denim trousers, to accompany my recently purchased fancy-dress accoutrements. I would have gone for black denim trousers, but I didn't have any, as I've always felt they are an unnecessary deviation from the classic blue hue. I tied the Zorro mask around my glasses and the neckerchief and cape around my neck. As this was my second attempt at the procedure, it was completed swiftly and with minimal fuss. I looked at my thinning grey hair and considered adding Zorro's hat into the mix to make the disguise impenetrable but didn't feel its extravagantly wide rim would emanate the gravitas befitting of Fairness Man's belief system. I figured my hair was pretty typical of many men in their later years so didn't feel it would expose me in any way. Just to be on the safe side, I located a thinsulate bobble hat from my winter clothing reserves. Its white crystal pattern blended with dark green was slightly off kilter with the rest of Fairness Man's outfit, but the sudden fear that someone would recognise my upper head started to consume me, so I put on the hat and that was that.

Fairness Man opened the garage door, placed his posterior on the comfortable brown leather padded seat and rode off into the unknown. As he hurtled down towards the high street, the nervous excitement pulsing, he heard a car honking and guess who was passing by; none other than the Swine, with his bushy eyebrows, stubby nose and inane bloody grin, clogging up the road in his motherfucking Land Rover. He slowed up and rolled down his window and uttered, in his inimitable bark, 'George, what's with the fancy dress? You look like a bloody freak, man.'

He'd been able to detect that Fairness Man was inhabiting the physical form of yours truly, George Barry. I should have known that with his military intelligence background, he would be trained to detect and expose dual identities. While he was mentally deficient in other areas, such as empathy, compassion, creativity, humour and diplomacy, he had one key strength that I had overlooked.

Thinking quick on his feet, Fairness Man responded with a metaphorical smokescreen to get the Swine off his scent (also metaphorical). He broke out into a thick Latin accent (don't ask why, his instincts are beyond the comprehension of us mere mortals) and replied, 'Zees iz not George. I cam all ze way from Venezuela.'

He was harnessing a new faith in the thespian craft with a vim and vigour, mining an oral cadence from deep within that was far removed from my sonorous Essex tones. Before the Swine was able to reply, Fairness Man was able to make a swift exit onto Oaks Avenue, out of harm's way. At this point, he was confident that his masterful use of Spanish, albeit using English words, had sowed the seed of doubt in the (as stated clearly earlier) mentally deficient corridors of the Swine's decrepit brain. After a couple of minutes, confident the coast would be clear, Fairness Man turned back out of Oaks Avenue, by now sweating profusely, particularly in the scalp region, nestled, as it was, within its bobble-hatted cocoon. Ignoring the head-based heat, he cycled at full tilt for approximately two to three minutes, before reaching Burhampton High Street.

There stood the American coffee shop whose name will not pass my lips. Fairness Man parked the Raleigh outside. He noticed that the hypnotised corporate-worshipping drones sat in a line by the window, on ergonomically deficient stool-highchair hybrids, had moved their heads away from their phones and were looking him up and down. Some looked incredulous while others smiled. Fairness Man was more than happy to add a dose of humour to proceedings. While social justice was a serious issue, there was room for a jet stream of fun to help propel it along its virtuous way. A woman who looked in her late twenties, hair cut in a jagged fringe and wearing angular red specs, raised her phone to take a picture. Yes, Fairness Man was already resonating with the young, and it dawned on him the potential social-media impact he could have. The Burhampton Forum aside, I rarely set foot near social media. Except for my dormant Facebook account, I was a non-participant in the digital social domain, but I had a feeling this was about to change. I will be contacting Sophie forthwith to get the latest guidance on a world which, to be perfectly honest, I find incredibly irritating. In the old days, you might sometimes have to endure flicking through someone's holiday snaps or listen to how well dear Johnny was doing at school, during that social convention known as a dinner party. Now, if you were so inclined, you can have this sort of self-centred slop digitally spewed into your eyes day or night, courtesy of some emotionally repressed billionaire geeks who've sold their souls and your identities to the devil. The absolute fuckers. First a thespian détente, and now a social media entente cordiale, and Fairness Man is not even hours old. I could see that there was going to be a natural tension borne out of our differing belief systems, but with my diplomatic arsenal at the ready, we could make our relationship work. I'm a master of finding common ground while also being able to toe the line. Fairness Man will find me a pleasure to work with. I may even introduce a 360 appraisal system for both parties to help us strive for continual improvement. I think I'll look for a macro-economist with complementary HR experience, once the necessary funds are available.

Fairness Man walked into the coffee shop and surveyed the environment. Without a fully fleshed strategy he relied on his instincts and embarked on what I will call a smash and grab. Using a split-second system of demographic profiling he swooped and took what, I'm guessing, were an Americano and a skinny latte from a couple in a similar or slightly older age bracket to myself, on the basis that he was wearing mustard cords (a crime in its own right) and she was wearing those annoying slip-on shoes with the gold buckle on the front, the type that are favoured by pseudo-aristocratic morons. What Fairness Man hadn't calculated was the response of who we shall now refer to as Mustard Cord Man. After his coffee was swiped from under his nose, he stood up and started to chase Fairness Man around the shop. For a man who looked like his idea of exercise was taking an extra-long shit, he could certainly shift his ample body at a considerable rate.

'What are you doing, you fucking imbecile!' he screamed like a madman.

'Redistributing the nation's wealth, you corduroyed fuckwit,' was Fairness Man's well-crafted retort.

As Fairness Man sprinted around the edge of the coffee shop, cup in each hand, trying not to spill a drop, he strategically knocked over a chair in the path of Mustard Cord Man, sending him tumbling to the floor. Fairness Man was not to be outdone by anyone with such a regressive class-signalling dress sense. Oh no. As he left, he noticed that the woman with the red angular glasses still had her phone fixed on the action, and he could see from her relaxed yet engaged body language that he was still resonating with the millennial demographic. No doubt she was streaming the action straight into the epicentre of the digital political maelstrom. A maelstrom that Fairness Man was born to be part of. In the ideal world, he would like to have obtained more than two coffees but realised in this modern, shallow, far from ideal image-based existence, it was the symbolism of his actions that mattered most. In time, we will refine our methods and be able to increase our haul, but for now, Fairness Man will knowingly but regrettably play to the masses like a fine-tuned fiddle or an intellectual radical circus performer (note to self – consider how radical circus can change the hearts and minds of middle England to accept a vision for social utopia).

He placed the Americano and latte into the trailer, nestled betwixt the fragrant and freshly cleaned white towels (I would need to construct a good excuse for their inevitable coffee-stained appearance once they re-emerged into Nancy's efficient yet officious laundry system) and it dawned on him that he had forgotten to obtain takeaway cups to facilitate efficient transportation. Looking back into the shop, he could see Mustard Cord Man was back on his feet and heading for the door. Fairness Man would have to rely on his excellent natural balance to minimise coffee spillages en route to Larton. This was just the sort of adverse conditions in which he thrived. He got on the Raleigh, raised a defiant fist and left Mustard Cord Man shouting garbled invectives, which he blocked out as he cycled on his path of redistribution.

Head down, legs pumping, he imagined it was a time trial in Le Tour. He warmed to the idea of being an elite athlete as the pace ratcheted up to a level I had never previously experienced. A younger George Barry was no slouch on two wheels and was even what you might describe as a bit tasty, but this was on an entirely different plateau or strata.

Fairness Man arrived in Larton and pulled up to inspect the trailer. He had not foreseen the impact of his electric pace. Both coffee cups had endured approximately 60–70% liquid spillage. At this point, George Barry would have spiralled into a defeatist gloom, but not Fairness Man. My valiant alternative persona saw the lack of coffee as an opportunity. He simply mixed the two drinks together to make a new unnamed caffeinated concoction. Cape wafting in the breeze, he strode up to the village green, empty bar a professional dog walker – a middle-aged woman with red frizzy hair and a wild look in her eyes, the look of someone who had been worn down by the daily canine onslaught of barks, yelps, dry humping

41

and shit. Fairness Man saw an opportunity to help one of the oppressed, belittling herself with the menial work of the rich. He approached the dog walker, dropped one knee to the ground and offered her the cup of coffee as a symbol of the ongoing class war. An energetic Weimaraner jumped up in excitement and placed his front legs on Fairness Man's shoulders. He took this as blessing from the animal kingdom for his endeavours, a primal pagan sign condoning his principles and approach to fiscal policy in the post-industrial age. The put-upon dog walker yanked the lead of the unruly hound and looked down at Fairness Man's masked face. What happened next is as close to a spiritual experience that is possible for an atheist operating at the peak of his sentient abilities.

The dog walker took the cup and had a sip, to which she stated, 'I prefer a cappuccino, but thanks, it's a lovely thought. Have a nice day,' before placing it back in Fairness Man's hands.

She smiled the smile of someone who realised they were part of something monumental, before her attention switched to the pressing need of clearing up the newly arrived faeces of a cockapoo. The seed of change had been planted; the revolution had truly begun.

Emboldened, Fairness Man made an about-turn and made his way to the Raleigh. Legs tired, he dug deep and battled the lactic acid as he returned to something approaching the blazing pace reached on the outward journey. He decided on taking the long route back home. He didn't want to risk the possibility of a heavy police presence. He cycled over the river that separated the two villages and felt a triumphant glow as he passed the

'Welcome to Burhampton' road sign. As he zigzagged through the quiet backstreets his heart rate dropped and his physiology returned to normality. It was as if his work was done for today and he was slowly leaving my body. While my adulation for his overall abilities and specifically his leg strength was sky-high, I don't think I could deal with his presence twenty-four hours a day. It would undoubtedly lead to burnout, which would be disastrous for the daily running of my operations. I was in this for the long game and that meant keeping my brain and body in good working order. Before turning into Elm Lane, he dismounted the Raleigh and crouched down behind a handily placed Porsche Cayenne. He removed mask, cape, neckerchief, and sweat-drenched woolly hat, carefully placing them under my black sweatshirt. At last I've found something positive about the oversized status-driven metallic cubes of planetary destruction. Getting back to my feet, I felt dizzy as the last strains of Fairness Man left my body. Thanks, buddy, I couldn't have done it without you.

There was still the conspicuous trailer attached to the Raleigh, which could raise a red flag (as both a socialist symbol and a warning sign) to the whereabouts of the new left-wing superhero working the streets of Burhampton. However, I was prepared to take the risk. Nobody would ever expect a mild-mannered chap like myself being complicit in the machinations of the one and only Fairness Man. OK, other superheroes may have quashed greater foes than Mustard Cord Man but you know the old saying, 'Nothing worse than a greedy, bigoted, entitled right-wing fanatic scorned'. What he lacked in the physical department, he more than made up for with his bloody-minded, pig-headed belligerence. I shall be filing away the image of his defeated vein-popping head to the cabinet of glee.

Back on the Raleigh, I successfully navigated the last turn of the journey, gliding into Elm Lane, up the drive and, in one fluid movement, dismounted and swung open the garage doors. Once safely inside Barry Towers, I picked up the two mugs which bore the mark of the American coffee shop. I took them to the shed and, with hammer in hand, unleashed my hatred on the china scum, before placing the broken pieces in the kitchen bin, which was only what they deserved for being ceramic udders dangling from the corporate cash cow. I finished off proceedings by playing a rare live version of 'Walk On By' by Dionne Warwick from my treasured vinyl collection. I bet Mustard Cord Man had wished he'd walked on by and not have faced the might of Fairness Man.

Bobby was moping in the kitchen. I could tell he was put out that he hadn't been included in the day's events. I think he had a growing animosity for this Fairness Man chap, who was muscling in on his patch. Bobby needed to feel important and have a role to play in the overthrow of the system. I knew his ethos had evolved beyond basic pack instincts and, through osmosis, he had acquired deep-seated beliefs in equality, public-sector ownership of utilities, the collective bargaining power of trade unions and a progressive model for asset redistribution. Through his unwavering companionship, attentive listening and keen eye for detail, he had contributed, in kind, to my vision for the future. Fear not, Bobby, I won't betray you. I shan't be shipping you to Mexico, where you'll meet a bloody and fatal blow to the head from a pickaxe.

Feeling exhausted from the morning's events, I made my way upstairs for a tactical nap, but no sooner had my head hit the pillow than my phone started ringing. I'd recently spent two productive and informative hours changing my ringtone. However, somehow I'd downloaded the wrong file, and rather than the beautiful Bacharacian melody of 'Raindrops Keep Falling on My Head' – Redford and Newman holed up with a beautiful dame, revelling in the joys of the humble pushbike, before heading to Mexico, where they'll meet a bloody and fatal barrage from the surrounding infantry – I'd ended up with 'Gangnam Style'. Until this point I hadn't made the parallels between Trotsky and *Butch Cassidy and the Sundance Kid*. If dear Lenny had lived to a ripe old age, he may have enjoyed hunkering down with some popcorn to watch the classic Western. I'm not sure how he would have resolved his inherent distrust of the western imperialist scum with enjoying some of Hollywood's finest performers. Perhaps, like me, he would have tolerated such entertainment as a reinforcement of the infantile nature of capitalism, pumping out dumbed-down versions of the USA's paltry history. Alas, we will never know.

As the Korean technopop filled my tired mind, I reluctantly picked up my phone and saw Nancy's name emblazoned on its screen. She was about to drop an almighty bombshell. She had been taking a well-earned break from her conserving when none other than Liz Swine had sent her a video clip of Fairness Man evading the sweaty mitts of Mustard Cord Man. For fuck's sake, what's wrong with these bloody Swines? Can't they just leave people to go about their societal crime fighting in peace? It transpired that the video, most likely filmed by the well-intentioned millennial in the angular red glasses, had made its way via Twitter, #crazycoffeedude, onto the *Larton Gazette*'s website, 'Man in Black Mask in Daylight Coffee Robbery', aspersions cast, and theories expounded in the comments section, before it arrived into the epicentre of the Burhampton Forum. Nancy, just like every-bloody-one else, was pointing the finger at me.

At this point, I had to explain, at length, that while it may have looked like me, it was in fact Fairness Man, and wherever he forged his path to an ethically sound society, I would follow. Nancy did question the ethics of stealing, in her words, 'taxpayers' coffee', but I gave a pithy yet intellectual robust explanation for why Fairness Man's behaviour was not only justified but essential to stop society creeping towards a super-rich stranglehold which will starve the planet of the metaphysical and literal oxygen we need and lead to the downfall of the human race.

Nancy recommended I have a nice lie-down – oh, for Pete's sake. I think she may be questioning my sanity. I'm not going mad. How hard is it to grasp the fact that I've created an alter ego who will, I hope, in time, take responsibility for his own actions? On top of that, what he is doing is right and proper. If only I had the wit, guile and fleet of cycling foot, I would be happy to take the credit. But this time, comrades, it was dear old Fairness Man at the helm.

I opened my laptop with trepidation, as I readied myself to enter the putrid bog that is the Burhampton Forum. No surprises who was at the front of the highly opinionated and judgemental queue; you've guessed it, fucking Swinster. In what I would describe as remedial English, typical of someone who has spent a career in military 'intelligence', he ridiculed my Spanish accent, before putting my strange behaviour down to either a breakdown or perhaps a neurological condition. He used the usual get-out-of-jail card of the privileged yet thick, that he was no expert.

Wilko (Chinny) chipped in at this point and vouched for my *upstanding yet eccentric personality*. Oh, how the entitled play the benevolent hand while simultaneously belittling the efforts of the tired and oppressed.

I had to enter a power trance, lasting forty to fifty seconds, to neutralise the inner rage that was brewing. When the time permits, I shall document, trademark, disseminate and propagate this concentrated, high-intensity wellbeing technique. Burhampton would be a different place if its citizens tapped into some of the mental processes that I embed into my daily rituals. As I contemplated creating a Burhampton Forum profile for Fairness Man, RevRightOn piped up and unleashed a string of religiously indoctrinated, rabid Islamophobia.

He began, '*I do not know this George Barry character, but I have good reason to believe that he is an undercover ISIS operative. Unfortunately for him, his cover is blown. I shall be notifying the local constabulary as soon as I can drag myself away from this riveting discussion. I would like to reassure anyone who is feeling disturbed or anxious, or quite possibly both, about today's events, that God loves you and you are all welcome in St Mary's Church. Please visit our website www. godisgreat-stmarys.co.uk for more information.*'

Not only is Reverend Ormerod a racist; he is a shameless opportunist to boot, praying on the vulnerable in the desperate attempt to get an extra few quid in his tainted collection box.

The thought of the local police paying a visit filled me

with dread. I don't think having an ethical yet borderline maverick alter ego would fit within their narrow interpretation of the law. In their traditional binary world of cops and robbers, theft would be theft. If only they could arrest the politicians who are stealing our futures and imprisoning our minds in a neo-crypto-techno-feudalism. As my anxiety rose, I contemplated fight or flight. George Barry, out of practicality and not cowardice, would often flee terror, but with Fairness Man on board, I could combine my more natural defensive state with his unique brand of offensiveness. I could have my hardwired genetic cake and eat it. What this amounted to in layman's terms, was a decision to retreat from my cosseted western lifestyle and to place myself amongst the homeless. From this vantage point, Fairness Man could launch further forays into the community, mobilising the disillusioned and dispossessed.

I acted fast, wanting to get out before Nancy's return. Thankfully, I'm a keen and able camper. In my well-worn Millets backpack, still bearing the traces of mud from my last yomp, I placed a green domed tent, a couple of changes of clothes, a gas burner, a sleeping bag, a torch, two tins of low-sugar baked beans, an army surplus water canteen, cutlery, my Swiss army knife, fifty pounds in cash, and, last but not least, Fairness Man's attire. While my sudden and unannounced departure would come as a shock to Nancy, I tried to lessen the blow with a well-crafted note.

Nancy, while I love you and cherish the many years we have spent together under a safe roof, I must now depart for the foreseeable future. No, to put your mind at rest, there isn't another woman. My mistress is the socialist cause. *The allure of her basic tenets of equality, workers' rights and state ownership of essential utilities is too great for me to resist. You are now aware of Fairness Man. He will accompany me, providing the support and moral fortitude I need in my quest. While this may all appear 'crazy' and out of character, I can assure you I'm as sane as I've always been. It's from my actions that I aim to support those with real mental health challenges. As Fairness Man has now broken into the social-media world and created a stir, I have no doubt you will see him again. When you do, you can rest in the knowledge that I am safe and well. Unfortunately, Reverend Ormerod has got it into his warped brain that I'm an ISIS operative, so be prepared for a visit from the police. Please tell them that I've gone to visit my brother in Australia. All very spur-of-the-moment, blah, blah, blah. That should get them off my scent. I shall leave with you my phone, as I'm going fully off grid. I had meant to ask Sophie for some social-media advice on her visit next weekend. If she has ideas how Fairness Man can further boost his profile, that would be most appreciated. When I return, the world will be a better place.*

All my love,

George

As I went to say farewell to Bobby, it was too much to bear and decided that he would be a welcome companion in the many moments when Fairness Man was elsewhere. I think Nancy will soon get used to my absence, but if she was lumbered with that smelly mutt (her choice of words, not mine), the locks may be changed and the divorce papers in the post. There will be no address for her to send the divorce papers, so that at least gives me cause for comfort.

Bobby sat contently in the cosy confines of the fur-lined pram, as I cycled into the woods that abut the North-East corner of Burhampton. The woods are easy to reach from Barry Towers without needing to travel on any main roads, thus reducing the odds of a chance encounter with enemy forces. I couldn't avoid the army of curtain twitchers that lurked in the socially repressed backstreets of Burhampton that I passed, but I had to take my chances.

The several acres of ancient woodland are a spiritual home to us both. They are our space, where we can find a moment of serenity away from the cut and thrust of village life. We knew every path, tree and shrub, like it was our own. As Bobby scampered on and away from the concrete conformity, I could see he was happy to spend a joyous night at one with mother nature. Once ensconced deep in the woods, Bobby and I found a clearing, where I pitched our tent and waited for night to descend.

As I pen this entry, cocooned in my quilted sleeping bag with Bobby by my side, the wind whipping the tent's plastic domed facade, I'm already missing Nancy's wonderful aura. I'm also missing the well-stocked fridge. My misgivings about the overspending on unnecessary treats, contributing to our single-use plastic footprint, soon dissolved as I fantasised about eating profiteroles with chocolate sauce. After the seismic events of the day, I made a note to myself to consider how the fair distribution of puddings and confectionery could form part of my masterplan.

THURSDAY APRIL 1ˢᵀ

It was April Fool's Day and practical jokes were off the menu. While the local woods had served their purpose for the first night on the run, they left us isolated. It is this sort of social isolation that the underclass experience every day. I needed to focus my attention on the dispossessed, hear their grievances and right their wrongs. Burhampton didn't have, as far as I was aware, any dispossessed; not unless the Spatchcockers get their way and oust Abdul from The Golden Tandoori. Weyford, approximately nine miles due west of Burhampton, population 23,000, twinned with Aarschot in Flanders and winner of the most Well-Kept Town Award 2007, had a growing enclave of homeless people. On a recent trip, I spotted a tent in the memorial gardens. I'm on good information that the local council, Women's Institute and the Rotary Club are up in arms about what they are describing as an 'invasion of the undesirables'.

The humble tent has become a symbol of inequality that some just can't bear to see. Well, Weyford, there's one more tent heading your way, so you'd better get used to it.

I shared a can of cold baked beans with Bobby. He seemed to take great joy in their tomatoey goodness. They were undoubtedly a taste sensation compared to the dehydrated crap he ingested on a daily basis. I once tried one of the dried biscuity things he eats, and I can report that it was vile. With our bellies sated, I packed up and we made our way to Weyford. I considered that the old bill may be looking for me after yesterday's events, but one advantage of the woeful funding of the police force was that their resources are spread so thin that the chances of them tracking me down were slim.

As I cycled in the early spring sunshine, I felt a wave of tranquillity rush over me. I was shedding the layers of conventional living, rendering me free to fight the good fight unimpeded. Admittedly, there were certain drawbacks, such as lack of easy access to flushing toilet facilities and the internet, but I'd get used to these mild annoyances. I'm sure when Lenny was exiled in Switzerland, he had to do without what he would have classified as bourgeois indulgences, but he didn't let it get him down. Much like myself, he was too busy constructing his theories and vision to get bogged down in such trivialities. As a celebration of my liberty, the open road, the cause, the workers (take your pick, comrades), I quelled any yearning for home comforts and broke into my £50 of cash reserves to invest in a bag of Percy Pigs from dear old M&S. Their gelatinous, sugary joy kept Bobby and me in high spirits as we made our way to Weyford. We soon penetrated the outer suburbs, which rolled by in well-kept monotony.

On reaching Weyford city centre, we circumnavigated the consumerist glass-walled prison better known as The Meadows and arrived at the memorial gardens. I wheeled in the Raleigh and trailer, as I'd neglected to bring my sturdy D-lock. It has a security rating of four stars and easily repels the wandering eye of the errant bike thief.

In the far corner of the gardens, nestled in the bushes behind the cafe and toilets, was a red, standard-issue, domed tent. I felt a strange sensation as if Fairness Man was stood behind me, tapping my shoulder. He was nagging, imploring, let's face it, downright begging to get back in the action. Of course, he was right, I couldn't hold him back for a moment longer. Leaving Bobby tied up outside, I entered the public toilets ready to transform. Every sinew of my body morphed into something new, fierce and unfathomable as I put on the mask, cape and neckerchief. It was reminiscent of *American Werewolf in London* but without the fangs and excessive body hair. I decided against wearing the bobble hat, to avoid another uncomfortable bout of scalpel sweating, and tucked it into my belt for safe-keeping.

As Fairness Man left the toilet cubicle, he was faced with a man and a young boy, who was about two or three years old. The infant gave Fairness Man a look that said, while not fully cognisant of the fact, he knew he was in the presence of greatness. One day, my child, you will look back on this as the defining moment of your formative years. With no time or need to explain himself to the man and child, Fairness Man departed the toilets, untied Bobby and made his way to the red plastic dome that lay yonder.

What I hadn't accounted for was Bobby's reaction to

Fairness Man. In my haste, I had overlooked the fact that my canine companion had yet to be exposed to him. I'm no dog psychologist but I deduced that anxiety brought on by the displacement of his master (me, George Barry), combined with the conflicted instant adoration he had for Fairness Man, set him off in what can only be described as an uncharacteristic violent episode.

Bobby launched himself at Fairness Man's left leg and sunk his teeth into his thigh. In my agony, my mind flitting back and forth between my two identities, I let out a howl, followed by a gentle whimper that Bobby instinctively recognised as his dear old George. As blood dripped down my leg, I contemplated the wonder of the unbreakable bond we have. Fairness Man had no time for such petty sentimentality and, with a dismissive flick of the wrist, swept it aside.

'To inhabit suffering is to inhabit life,' he proclaimed to a couple of women, enjoying a mid-morning beverage, accompanied by delicious-looking chocolate brownies.

Fairness Man procured some serviettes from a stainless-steel dispenser on the table where the two women sat and masterfully dabbed the wound in an attempt to stem the flow of blood. One of the women kindly offered him a plaster, which he accepted with dignity. Thank the lord that there is some sense of community spirit left in this backwater.

With the wound under control and Bobby returning to a state of calm, he marched into the flowerbeds towards the red tent.

Once at the tent, he contemplated the correct etiquette for announcing his arrival. While he was a man of action, he was not a brute, and was mindful of personal space and privacy. With a knock on the door, a wrap of a knocker or the buzz of the bell all rendered infeasible, he vouched for a direct voice-based approach.

'Hello, is anyone home? It's a matter of great political and social importance,' he asked, in a polite yet dynamic tone.

This was met with a series of barely audible grunts and groans. The primitive sounds of a human who had got used to a more elemental existence. Fairness Man listened to the beautiful swish of the zip as the tent door opened. It spoke to his new-found nomadic existence. A young woman with wild brown curly hair and half-opened bloodshot eyes appeared from the tent. Her pallid skin was dotted with red spots and she wore a functional grey tracksuit top and matching bottoms.

What followed was a short exchange of views that he felt were both stimulating and enlightening. The young woman's name was Rose, and she had been sleeping rough, on and off, for the last two years. Fairness Man sensed her pain and felt compelled to offer her his support. He explained his recent initiative for caffeine-based wealth distribution to see if it would gain any traction, but it was apparent that Rose was most in need of vodka, not overpriced coffee. After less than twenty-four hours living as a homeless person, he sympathised with the need to self-medicate. He could quite easily fall foul to the throes of suffering, but his superhuman dynamism efficiently slayed negativity, so all that was left was an essential golden nugget of empowerment shining like a beacon wherever he went. This was not something that could be learnt; it was an innate strength buried deep within his psyche. The world's leading therapists and psychiatrists could try to unravel his genius and map his mental genome, but it would be outside the realms of conventional science.

Fairness Man decided he could quite easily switch caffeine for alcohol. One woman's double-shot skinny latte is another woman's mid-morning high-strength lager. He was prepared to support a dependence on alcohol as a stepping stone to socialist enlightenment. He hadn't buttoned down the detail, but he was thinking of some sort of mash-up of Alcoholics Anonymous's twelve stages to recovery and *Das Kapital*. He was a big-picture kind of guy and didn't like to get bogged down in logistics. Budgets, timing plans and spreadsheets were anathema to his instinctive flow. He felt that in a former life he was most probably a falcon, hovering in the thermals before swooping down on its ideologically opposed pray. My psyche, on the other hand, was far too nuanced to be boiled down to your traditional one-for-one reincarnation. I was most likely a combination of a workhorse, strong and steady, ploughing the fields, with the sprinkling of a wise owl, to account for my intellect, and the caring social values of the domestic cat. Even in the annals of ancient mythology a creature like this hadn't been imagined. It was through these undefinable characteristics that I was going to change the world.

Rose soon grew tired of his presence and requested to be left alone to contemplate the day ahead.

Her exact words were, 'Leave me alone, you fucking nutter. I don't need this right now,' but I put her aggressive manner down to going cold turkey, desperately craving her next fix of hard booze.

Fairness Man, ever the optimist, turned this lack of willingness to collaborate on a long-term strategy to empower the destitute and dispossessed, into a positive. He would win Rose over by providing some freshly procured artisan liquor.

He decided to shift tactics and redistribute wealth and assets through progressive street art taxation. Yes, it could be what you would classify as busking but with an underlying political foundation, mission and vision that elevated it to a high art form. While Fairness Man, like George Barry, had never previously dabbled with performance art, he was unfazed. He got on his bike and cycled up towards the entrance to The Meadows, where the happy yet ignorant shoppers of Weyford went about their days. He placed his bobble hat on the ground, ready to acquire cash, and began to perform. Bobby sat guard by the hat, understanding the importance of this fundraising activity. Fairness Man mimed a ceiling moving slowly down, crushing the spirits of the working classes. As he crumpled into the concrete floor, he sprung back to his feet and seamlessly shifted into a contemporary dance routine representing global warming. As the temperature rose and ice caps melted, he took off items of clothing. Bobby joined in by barking wildly and chasing his tail. It was obvious that his anxiety was overflowing in the face of the environmental crisis. As Fairness Man whipped off his trousers and performed the dance of a dying polar bear in his pants, the crowds grew to somewhere in the region of seven or eight. He shifted theatrical gears once more and started reciting some extemporised poetry on the housing crisis. All was going well, until he stumbled trying to think of a word to rhyme with opus. Not one to dwell on mishaps, he beautifully flowed straight into what he is now calling his anthem. Singing to the tune of 'Do You Know the Way to San Jose', he paraphrased his favourite quotes from Karl Marx. That he could merge 19th century political critique with late sixties easy listening, was testament to his intellectual and creative prowess.

As the sweet sounds of Dionne Warwick wafted in his mind and collided with my coherent vision for a better world, it felt good to be alive. Taking in the applause, he thanked his attentive audience and, hat in hand, collected a grand total of £2.12. He was pleased with this first attempt at fundraising. While it didn't stretch to a locally crafted bottle of gin, it covered the cost of a couple of cans of extra-strength cider from the conveniently located Booze Warehouse that was on the opposite side of the road to The Meadows. With his energy levels ebbing, he also acquired a reasonably priced packet of Bombay Mix, making use of our survival fund, which still ran to over £40. The spicy joy of eating the crunchy curried peanuts, peas and tubular items that bear no name, provided the fuel that propelled him back to the memorial gardens.

Once back in the gardens, Fairness Man felt that my superior diplomatic skills were better suited to the scenario. I have the common touch necessary to instigate an outreach programme for the homeless of Weyford. While lacking the athleticism, bravery and performance ability of Fairness Man, I have excellent interpersonal skills and an in-depth knowledge of diplomatic tactics acquired through a lifelong obsession with Henry Kissinger. If I could inject between 2–5% of Kissinger's negotiating chromosomes into my bloodstream, then we could rest assured that the future was in safe hands.

Entering the park toilets and the safe haven of cubicle number three, Fairness Man removed his mask and I re-emerged tired and in desperate need of a wash and shave. I sat down on the toilet for a well-deserved breather but could hear Bobby's lonely bark distracting me from my hygiene needs. While he is a friend and servant, he can stray into being needy sometimes. It's not his fault that he has evolved as a pack animal and has acute separation anxiety. Making full use of the soap dispenser, I had a gentlemen's wash of my face, pits and nether regions. Shaving would have to wait for another day, as I didn't have the necessary apparatus to hand, but I noted that the stubble, reminiscent of José Mourinho in his pomp, gave me an appearance more suited to a man of a homeless persuasion. Mask, hat, cape and cider in hand, I walked out to dear Bobby. His barking stopped as his anxiety was quelled. The yin of man and the yang of dog, as we walked side by side into the undergrowth.

After several attempts to call Rose out of her tent, it became obvious that she was elsewhere. In her desperate plight, she had hit the streets in a quest for an alcohol hit. I realised that to build a rapport with Rose, I needed to get in tune with the rhythms of homeless life. I needed to break down the psychological and physical barriers we place around us, shielding us from true feeling and manifesting in what I'm coining The Empathy Gap. A gap of understanding for the fellow human, which atomises behaviour and leaves the capitalist technocratic oligarchs free to control, manipulate and profit from our isolated existence. I think there is a book and workshop in the idea – feedback most welcome, comrades.

I set up camp ten metres to the left of Rose, as a show of solidarity but without wishing to impose on and threaten her hard-fought territory. As my first step towards closing The Empathy Gap (I will file for a TM in due course), I opened one of the cans of super-strength cider and glugged the cheap, sugary liquid down. Left on my own, away from the white noise of Burhampton, I felt a joyful glow inside. I lay down on my sleeping bag and drifted into a blissful sleep.

I woke in the late afternoon to Bobby licking my face. It was very handy living in the memorial gardens, as I was able to give him a walk around its leafy parameters. Bobby took particular interest in the duck pond, chasing up to the edge of the water and scaring off its avian residents. I needed to get him some dog food before his hunting instincts take over and he dines on mallard. Returning to my tent, I encountered Rose, who gave me a funny look, perhaps due to my striking resemblance to Fairness Man, albeit without mask and cape. I fetched the remaining can of cider and presented it as a peace offering. Rose stared at the can, wary of my intentions, but before I could embark on a well-crafted tribute to Fairness Man segueing into a broader sweep of my credo, aims and ethics, she was consuming its contents. I explained that my masked counterpart can sometimes overwhelm people with his superhuman aura, and that it was only natural for her to feel a degree of animosity.

She replied that, 'Wasn't it just you in a mask, you weirdo?'

This wasn't the first time I'd been called a weirdo, and

so it came as no surprise. I liked to be considered a weirdo as a vindication of my unconventional outsider status. I tried to explain that while Fairness Man may inhabit my body, we were separate physiological entities united in the people's struggle. We shared the same vision but had two complementary skill sets, personalities and pastimes. While I opted for a gentle stroll with Bobby, meditation, historical literature and easy listening jazz, Fairness Man favoured a vigorous spin class followed by the visceral blast of death metal. He was a man of instincts, while I was a man of learning and well-considered decision-making.

As Rose supped her cider, she became more attentive to my thoughts and opinions. I explained that my burgeoning political movement would provide her with the support she needed. Building for my heartland in Burhampton, we would help the rough sleepers, the addicts, the outcasts, find a way back into society. A path, a purpose, a sense of belonging and value. As a sweetener to the deal, I also offered a free trade agreement with the Barry Towers drinks cabinet. The cornucopia of untouched alcoholic beverages bought on a whim at Christmas and other miscellaneous social events, would provide a well-needed booze-laden bridge towards sobriety and societal integration. I didn't mention the Spatchcockers and their ilk but felt that Weyford was a good training ground for building up the necessary resilience needed when confronting their particular strain of self-serving ignorance. Rose seemed like she'd already built up a psychological pith helmet of resistance against what I shall pejoratively label arseholes. She will have her own label for such individuals, and through the support structure I will construct, I will not seek to dampen down her means of self-expression in the face of tyranny, prejudice and greed.

As Rose finished her can and walked away from our homeless enclave, I felt that I had planted the seed of change, which would sprout into a sapling of empowerment, before growing into a mighty oak of revolution. I set up my gas stove and heated up the remaining can of beans in celebration. Today, dear Bobby, we must feast, for tomorrow we carry on the fight.

FRIDAY APRIL 2ND

I woke as the sun rose over Weyford Memorial Gardens. The early morning joggers and dog walkers were in full flow, sending Bobby scampering in delight to explore his new paradise. I ventured to the local shops and treated myself to a finely baked croissant and freshly squeezed orange juice. For young Bobby, I acquired a can of hearty chunks of prime reconstituted jellied meat. He wolfed it down with gusto and gave me the look of a beast at peace with himself and the world around. In that moment he'd found an equilibrium, a higher state, a primal nirvana that humans could only imagine. As I tucked into the flaky sustenance of the croissant, I congratulated myself on the foresight I'd shown in placing Bobby at the centre of my political operations. There would always be room for his black fluffy face at the top table. While the Soviet Union may have sent a dog into space, they still stuck rigidly to an exclusive human political elite. We would not only dismantle homo sapien elitism, but we would welcome and incorporate an animal meritocracy into new-founded political institutions. I would need to work out a way of letting them voice their opinions that was both simple and coherent. If I can track down the modern-day equivalent of Doctor Doolittle, we'll be off and away.

Returning to my tent, I could hear Rose waking from her booze-addled slumber. The intermittent groans were punctuated with a rich palate of swearing: most probably brought on by the combination of a pounding headache and an acidic gut. The thought of Rose's alcohol-imposed plight brought me back to my wilder days, carousing the night spots of Basildon. Before Nancy took me under her beautiful and well-feathered wing, I was prone to over-indulgence. I'd willingly join the Friday-night throng, drinking themselves into oblivion as they battled with existential angst and social alienation. I winced as I thought back to a time when I woke up in a pool of my own urine, but on reflection, realise that this and several other stories of alcohol-drenched woe, were the raw experiences from which my world vision would emerge (thankfully not smelling of piss).

I sat patiently waiting for Rose to appear and initiated one of my longer-form meditation techniques. This style of total mind-cleansing would be the basis of a later chapter in my writings on the power of stillness in the class struggle. For a second, my resolve was tested, as my visualisation of a dappled glade in Epping Forest was invaded by an image of Nancy anxiously pacing the newly laminated kitchen floor, her slippers giving off a gentle squeak of despair. By now I'd been on the run for approximately thirty-five hours and would be on the radar of Surrey Police Force. Without my phone they had no way of using GPS to triangulate my whereabouts. Modern policing techniques are all well and good until you are dealing with an analogue native. A man equally versed in long-wave radio as he is with 5G internet transmission. I had a hunch that Fairness Man veered to the side of technological advancement over pure instinct and intuition. I sensed that he was itching for a WhatsApp chat or a bit of forum banter, but I'm sure a digital detox would enhance, not detract, from both his essence and aura. Free from the cyber-crutch of modern life, he was free to spread his able wings and fly headlong into the winds of progress. I felt bad that Nancy would be worrying about my safety. Don't fret, my sweet beacon of beauty, as soon as I get a chance, I'll send a message of hope that will allay your fears. By which method and medium I would send a message was, as yet, unclear. My first thoughts were of a homing pigeon gliding down onto the kitchen window ledge, catching Nancy's eye as she prepared poached egg on toast. With no immediate access to a feathered beast with navigational skills, this idea was a non-starter. With no easy solution presenting itself, I comforted myself in the knowledge that Nancy was built of sterner stuff and would soon get used to my absence. To be honest, I think she is probably enjoying the peace and quiet.

Rose crawled out of her tent, and before she could burst into an expletive-ridden rant, I presented a spare croissant I'd held in reserve. Rose accepted the French breakfast staple as a welcome antidote to her obvious physical discomfort. Seeking to capitalise on my generosity, I once again held out an olive branch in the form of relocation to Burhampton and a structured programme for reintegration into society. Rose explained that her long-term partner, Steve, had upped sticks a couple of weeks back and she was contemplating heading to London.

'I'll try my luck in the bright lights,' she said, not sounding sure of herself.

I threw in the Barry Towers drinks cabinet card once more, while also mentioning there was the possibility of a spare bed for her to rest her head. This, I admit, was a gamble, as Nancy may not be in a mood to accept me back over the threshold, let alone a woman of no fixed abode with a substance dependence and a multitude of as-yet-undiagnosed mental conditions. I will appeal to Nancy's benevolent nature and all will be fine. Any festering rage will dissipate once she understands the necessity of providing Rose care and support, as a vital step on the path to end the wealth-inequality continuum. Rose will be the necessary catalyst which will catapult Nancy headlong into the revolution. I may have to buy her a jaunty beret, so she feels the part.

As my mind wandered into these unchartered waters where ideology meets action, I remembered that Sophie and Nathan were coming to stay this weekend, which meant there would be no room at the inn. Thankfully there is a camp bed in the garden shed. I can vouch for its slim yet comfortable mattress, which I sometimes utilise when having a siesta out of view of Nancy and her ever-expanding list of chores. If it wasn't for the litany of odd jobs that are flung in my general direction, it would be unfathomable what I would be achieving on a daily basis. As it is, I'm still managing to hit monumental intellectual heights, firing on only a single cylinder of my ideological jet engine. Lenny didn't have such domestic impediments to hold him back. He just waited for the inevitable demise of the Russian royal family, mobilised the proletariat and the rest is history. I, on the other hand, must multi-task while trying to overcome the reluctant acceptance of the status quo by vast swathes of the populous.

Stomach replete with croissant and having been worn down by my attritional barrage of logic and clearly listed personal benefits, Rose seemed willing to give my rehousing and rehabilitation programme a try. Those years of tireless negotiations on the optimisation of administrative processes in Basildon Council Housing Department have not gone to waste. I explained that if she didn't take to life in Burhampton, I'd bring her straight back to Weyford. I was confident that once she'd enjoyed some of the comforts of life at Barry Towers, there would be no turning back. As I looked into her bloodshot eyes, I thought about the whereabouts of her family and why had she been left to fend for herself in this cruel world. I considered opening up this psychological can of worms, but while I can instil mindfulness into daily routines by plunging the well of stillness and resolve, my toolkit doesn't stretch to full-blown trauma. Fairness Man wouldn't be the man to turn to in such circumstances. His mind goes full tilt in the direction of action and so is unable to spot, let alone support, the nuanced and complex matters of the troubled mind. He kicked anxiety and depression defiantly in the butt, so it was hard for him to relate to those people who struggled with matters of the mind. Nancy had the emotional capacity to support and guide those in need.

While never voiced, I'm sure it was part of what drew her to me, as she single-handedly pulled me out of my world of binge-drinking and ready meals that subsumed my darker years, commonly known as the eighties. A decade that people gaze back at with rose-tinted specs, as they skip through a field of deely boppers serenaded by Limahl, airbrushing out the miners' strike, the decimation of the North and the demise of working-class identity. Nostalgia, you are a cruel mistress of deception.

Rose packed up her limited possessions. Besides her tent, sleeping bag, duvet, pillow and a meagre selection of clothes, there was nothing of note. No books, phone, photos or jewellery cluttered Rose's life. In her destitute state, she had stripped away the trappings of modern life and what remained was an ascetic existence close to the hunter-gatherers of old but placed in a world that valued acquisition and accumulation over care.

I led Rose to the ever-resilient Raleigh, which I wheeled out of a neighbouring bush. She eyed the vehicle with suspicion. I could see she was doubting this fine British-made bicycle's ability to transport two adults, a dog and their collective possessions. Affirmative action was needed to quell Rose's anxiety before she changed her mind. I rifled in my bag and grabbed my sartorial accoutrements to an alternate identity. I crouched down and made a commando roll into the gap in the bush that had previously housed the Raleigh. As I rose to my feet, I felt a twinge in my back. I had an affinity with an ageing Roger Moore as he tried to keep up with the physical strains of filming *For Your Eyes Only*. Roger made up for his lack of athleticism through a raised eyebrow and good dose of sex appeal, whereas I overcome the constraints of the ageing process through a hearty mix of denial and light stretching exercises. I must admit that the stretching had taken a back burner of late, but when time permits, I will integrate it back into my finely balanced schedule.

I snapped out of this moment of reflection on my mortality by putting on the mask, cape and neckerchief of the enigma that is Fairness Man. He doesn't dwell on physical impediment or ailments; in fact, I'm not sure if he has ever experienced any. The lower lumber pain dissipated as Fairness Man sprung to his feet and beckoned Rose over. He placed their possessions in the pram and put Bobby, who broke into an uncharacteristic fit of barking, on top. He was angry that he was downgraded to what was, to all intents and purposes, a second-class seat. Fairness Man dampened his rage by giving him the promise of a pit stop for a pack of Percy Pigs. While Bobby was easy to placate, there was a growing tension between Rose and Fairness Man that would be harder to overcome. Perhaps she was threatened by his gung-ho attitude or maybe she had a phobia of men in masks. Whatever it was, she clearly disliked him and pined for the return of the well-mannered and even-handed approach of my good self.

Fairness Man felt no animosity as he coaxed Rose onto the bike seat. Rising aloft on the pedals, he circled the bike out of the bushes and onto the path that meandered through the gardens, passed the gawping public. As he and Rose left the gardens and headed in the direction of Burhampton, the residents of Weyford breathed a collective sigh of relief that a couple of undesirables would soon be crossing over their borders and an imagined order of old

Albion would resume. A romanticised world of cricket on the village green and warm beer, before people of darker hues muddied their Great British waters. An introspective world of good old-fashioned ignorance and emotional repression. A happy time of conformity, acceptance and low life expectancy, where everyone knew their place. The populist nationalist view that smote the powerless and protected ingrained privilege.

As Fairness Man pumped his legs in time to his gentle humming of Kraftwerk's 'Autobahn', his aura glowed a little like the lad from the Ready Brek ads, but this time it was the warming thermals of socialism heating his body, rather than branded porridge oats. He was happy to have rescued one lost soul from the mire of the home counties commuter belt. Rose held tight to his waist as they made their way. She repeatedly requested he slow down, but it fell on deaf ears. While he was a natural-born alpha male, Fairness Man did struggle with multi-tasking. When he was engrossed in elite cardiovascular activity he had an inability to hear and, on occasion, see, which had potential risks when navigating busy junctions. Rose resorted to physical interaction and started jabbing him in the back while complaining that she felt sick. Fairness Man's ignorance to Rose's pleas backfired, when she vomited an alcohol soup over his treasured cape.

Thankfully, for all parties, they were approaching M&S, and Fairness Man wheeled the Raleigh into a vacant bike rack and dismounted his trusty steed. He took of his vomit-drenched cape, rinsed it with water from his canteen and placed it in one of the handy side pockets on my backpack. He felt exposed in its absence but knew that any negative feeling would soon waft away once a supply of Percy Pigs was procured. Rose slumped down and sat on the pavement by the Raleigh. She leant her head forward between her legs and breathed in slowly. In her poor mental and physical state, she was finding it a strain to keep up with the frenetic energy of Fairness Man. I can vouch for her that it isn't easy, even without having endured the physical ravages of years living on the streets. Bobby, ever attentive to anguish and suffering, nestled by Rose's side and provided the wonderful medicine of canine companionship. Leaving Rose to convalesce, Fairness Man went off to acquire the necessary supplies. On his return, Rose's eyes lit up when she spotted a pack of four mini pork pies. Find me someone, vegan and vegetarians aside, who doesn't like a mini pork pie and I'd have to question their sanity. Their exquisite combination of jelly, pork and pastry has brought me back from the brink of despair several times over the years. On May 12th, 2001, the tears welled in my eyes as the news broke of the passing of the great Perry Como. A solitary pork pie, nestled in the top-left corner of the fridge, gave a culinary perspective that played a vital part in coming to terms with the loss of the colossus of the easy listening genre.

When the opportunity arises, I shall be contacting the appropriate mental health bodies and charities to request the addition of pork pies (and possibly Tunnock's Teacakes – the jury's out on their longer-term benefits, so I'll add the caveat that research studies would need to be undertaken to corroborate their effects on mental wellbeing) to their list of accredited therapeutic tools and techniques.

A tinge of pink returned to Rose's cheeks as she consumed all four pies. Fairness Man was annoyed that he hadn't stipulated an upper limit on pork-pie consumption. He switched his attention to the Percy Pigs, popped two straight in his mouth and bathed in the intense sugar rush. Somewhere there is a food scientist who must be feeling very pleased with themselves. Rose was showing some reluctance to getting back on the saddle after her bout of travel sickness. The animosity between her and Fairness Man was starting to impact on the overarching stratagem, and, not for the first time, I felt that I needed to interject in the proceedings. With Rose expressing the full force of her vehement dislike for all Fairness Man stood for, he took flight to the rear north-west corner of the M&S building, where there was a handily located petrol station with adjoining public conveniences.

Entering the public toilet facilities, the stench of urine hit him like a bodily fluid-based sledgehammer, or perhaps what you could describe as a pisskrieg: a urine-based ground and air offensive, attacking your eyes and nasal cavities in equal measure. He took off his mask and I thanked him for his fine effort thus far. As I gathered myself, I took in the pungent odour and my mind was taken back to the South Stand urinals at Roots Hall. A fine example of concrete, aluminium and corrugated iron. Functional design for the beer-filled football fans of the Essex coast. Halcyon days, comrades, halcyon days.

Walking back, ready to engage with Rose's turmoil, I pictured myself as an Anglo-Saxon Kofi Annan ready to run the gauntlet of UN protocol. Yes, followers, I was side-lining Lenny for a post-modern apolitical master statesman. Sometimes it's necessary to plough the furrow of neutrality in order to achieve your goals.

Rose's demeanour appeared to improve on my return. She made enquiries into why I kept putting on that mask and 'acting like a complete fuckwit'.

She didn't seem to grasp the concept of dual identity, so I left her question unanswered. I explained that we would continue at a slow speed, of approximately 1.75 times walking pace. On handing her the Percy Pigs, she decided to give it one more go. She'd also started to bond with Bobby, who barked with delight as Rose hoiked her leg over the Raleigh frame and sat astride its cushioned seat.

I soldiered on, as we edged towards Burhampton. My calves burnt like buggery without a seat to take my weight. I contemplated sitting on Rose's lap to relieve my suffering but counted that out on several obvious factors, including sexual harassment, invasion of personal space and a bout of Percy Pig-induced flatulence that I was struggling to contain. Thinking fast on my pedal-balancing feet, I whipped out my rolled sleeping bag and placed it perpendicular on the top beam of the bike frame. I sat down and found it made for an excellent makeshift cushion. As the burning sensation in my calves dissipated, I settled into a happy rhythm on the flat terrain that stretched out ahead. Inspired by my favourite Latin dance, the samba, I constructed a sequence of pedal, freewheel, pedal, pedal, freewheel, interspersed with a subtle hip wiggle: just enough rhythmic movement to feel the gentle winds of Ipanema in my hair, while not losing balance or causing undue concern to the road-weary Rose.

I asked how Rose was feeling but was met with silence. I turned my head and saw she was looking wistfully into the distance across a neighbouring field. I imagined that the

73

rural life was something of a mystery to her. To be honest, my agricultural knowledge was limited and I would still classify myself as a townie. We were two people bound by the scars of urban decay, seeking out a new life in this quiet – well, relatively quiet if it wasn't for the relentless flow of unnecessary car journeys piercing through the heart of bucolic bless, while contributing to rising sea levels and mass extinction – and welcoming – well, it would be welcoming if it wasn't for a sizable percentage of the population being small-minded morons – corner of England. Rose, we will find you a place in this fair land, where you can take root and bloom into a bouquet of holistic rehabilitation.

After what seemed like an eternity but was nearer to one hour and forty-five minutes, we passed into Burhampton. I felt anxious to bump into any of its residents after my time on the run from the law. Fairness Man had launched me into the limelight and life was never going to be the same again. From now on, like all great leaders, I'd embrace the public glare, absorbing its power to reflect an aura of compassion and agency. To that end, I decided on a pit stop at Burhampton's social melting pot, The Fox and Hounds, was in order. I felt in need of a little of the old Dutch courage (I've never considered the Dutch a timid bunch, but I can't blame them for the desire for the occasional alcoholic confidence boost), and it would also provide an opportunity to raise a glass to welcome Rose to Burhampton. It came as no surprise that Rose was on board with this idea. Her face ashen and her body breaking into the sporadic shakes of alcoholic withdrawal, it was imperative to keep her bloodstream topped up.

In The Fox and Hounds we were greeted by the coarse yet tolerable publican Tony. His vein-strewn cheeks, shiny bald head and well-developed paunch fitted the part of a man ready to pull the pumps of his finest foamy beer.

Before I had a chance to order our drinks, he broke into a stream of rambling nonsense: 'Look what the cat dragged in – if it isn't our coffee-snatching superhero. You looked a right pillock in that clobber. Were you feeling alright? Don't nick any of my punters' drinks, will you now.'

I could not and did not respond to his comments. I ordered a double Bacardi and Coke for Rose, a pint of pale ale for myself, and a packet of pork scratchings for Bobby. As Tony handed me my change, he referred to me as Captain Cappuccino. While I quite liked this alliterative moniker, I wasn't going to stoop to his level of tabloid humour. I simply smiled, took the drinks, and sat down with Rose and Bobby.

I have been developing a mindfulness technique called transcendental cognitive fog, or 'cog fog' for short. It is a technique for the more experienced meditator, which allows you to place a forcefield around yourself and repel all negative energy. My mastering of 'cog fog' wasn't advanced enough to deflect the strange looks and laughter from the other people in the pub, who, thankfully, were none of my acquaintances.

I apologised to Rose that our celebratory moment was being ruined by the psychological invasion of the chattering classes, but she didn't seem the least bit aware or concerned. On the contrary, her mood brightened with every gulp of her double Bacardi and Coke, and she started to display a new side of her personality, that of the wily and weathered raconteur. While her tales of life on the streets were tinged with sadness, she seemed to enjoy sharing them. She explained how her relationship with her partner, Steve, often strayed into violence, with Rose normally coming off the worse. Why she tolerated a man who seemed to regularly give her a beating is hard to fathom. I did not quiz Rose on this puzzling interpersonal dynamic, leaving my wondering mind to try and seek an answer.

I think sharing her trauma was giving Rose a moment to elevate the pain. I was happy to sit back and be her emotional sponge, soaking up her sodden woe. I held back from giving any advice or what you may define as counselling, as domestic violence is most definitely not one of my areas of expertise. Nancy and I have had heated rows, but they've stayed within the realms of psychological warfare. I have been on the receiving end of many an emotional jab and been floored by one or two mental uppercuts at the hands of Nancy's forceful, discursive nature. But when all is done, I've dusted myself down, revived and ready to leap into the joyous foray of our matrimony.

After indulging Rose for a good ten to fifteen minutes, I tried to steer the conversation back to more comfortable territory by asking her views on diversity and representation of minority opinions in the media, but it didn't seem to pique much interest. I think that some form of basic education needs to be factored into her rehabilitation and reintegration programme, the elements of which were starting to take shape. Yes, there were a few gaps in my thinking, but Rose is the vital guinea pig that I need. Not that I'm saying that Rose has as little value as a guinea pig or a guinea pig is of little value, for that matter. No, I follow the Buddhists on this one. We all have equal worth, well, up to a point. Buddha even included mosquitos as our equals, which is a step too far. I'm happy to advocate the killing of those buzzy, disease-carrying little bastards, who single-handedly destroyed our honeymoon to the Maldives. Nancy's bitten and blotchy legs are my abiding memory of what was supposed to be the romantic zenith of our relationship. How we managed to conceive Sophie on that fateful trip was a feat of perseverance through discomfort. These memories, compounded by the carbon footprint of long-haul travel, have crushed the desire for a repeat trip to the tropics.

Rose requested another drink, but I could sense that Bobby was getting restless. He knew that home was near and was most likely pining for a return to his usual staple diet of high-nutrition kibbles, with a treat on good behaviour. The pub visit had acted as something of a delaying tactic for our return to Barry Towers. I needed to take on my new-found responsibility and return home with my head held high. Sophie and Nathan were due over, with an ETA of 4–6pm based on previous visits, and I was hoping all would be smoothed over with Nancy in time for their arrival.

I led a reluctant Rose and an enthusiastic Bobby from our table towards the outdoors, while utilising 'cog fog' to block out the mindless verbal salvos that were spilling out of Tony's mouth. Rose, who had more imminent needs than learning advanced mindfulness techniques, was less tolerant. As I had enforced 'cog fog' I was not fully sentient but will relay a potted and potentially inaccurate version of events which, let's be honest, has become somewhat the norm in modern reportage. From what I can gather, Tony made a comment that Rose was my 'new bit on the side' – a phrase rarely uttered since 1988. I'm sure in other circumstances she would be happy to be incorrectly identified as my mistress. In fact, despite the age gap, she may even define me as a good catch, but rightly so, Rose took a dislike to Tony's regressive misogyny.

While I find confrontation a complex maze to be carefully navigated, Rose took a more direct approach. She responded by calling Tony a 'fat baldy fuck face' and finding a handily placed half-drunk pint of beer on an empty table, she flung it straight into his red, blotched face. From there on in, things get a bit sketchy, but when an octogenarian have-a-go hero tried to block Rose as she headed behind the bar to extend her attack on Tony, I knew it was time to interject. The octogenarian was a short, wiry fellow, with a hooked nose and the inch-deep wrinkles of a man who'd grafted through the decades. I pictured him as a young chimney sweep, a champion jockey, followed by a successful spell as a double-glazing salesman in Swanage. I felt the desire to test the accuracy of my vocational conjecture but resisted the urge.

He explained that, 'While I may be old, these hands are still tasty.'

Rose paid this short shrift, averting his 'tasty' hands with a quick sidestep, before launching herself on Tony and wrestling his substantial frame to the ground. Sitting on top of his large stomach, she slapped his bald head as if it was a tightly skinned bongo drum, providing percussive accompaniment to the synthetic pop piping through the pub's speaker system. I bent down and prised apart the grappling pair. I reapplied 'cog fog' to block out extraneous thoughts, as I restrained and removed Rose from the premises.

While our sojourn to The Fox and Hounds had been less than successful, Rose seemed visibly buoyed by the experience.

Head up, chest puffed, she proclaimed that she'd put 'that baldy inbreed in his place'.

I hadn't given much thought to Tony's gene pool until now, but I could see her point. He did have the gormless expression of a man whose ancestors hadn't cast their reproductive net very far.

Bobby was happy to be back outside, his nose sniffing in the direction of home. It had come to the point where Barry Towers beckoned, with its promise of cosy sofas and clean pants. Back on the Raleigh, we headed yonder and in a couple of minutes arrived home. As we glided down the empty driveway, the Vauxhall Astra conspicuous in its absence, I felt relieved that Nancy was out on one of her many weekly engagements. We entered the house and I breathed in its comforting floral bouquet; it had a clarity of pure air-freshened scent, from not having had to compete with Bobby's canine vapours.

After a mere two nights and two days on the road the quiet, clean environment felt alien. It was as if I'd been rewired as a nomad, at odds with the comforts of modern living. I filled Bobby's bowl to the brim and took a tentative step back into domesticity by making Rose and me a nice cuppa and some toasted white bread dripping in butter. Rose seemed happy with her new surroundings, describing our home as 'a bit posh'. I was uncomfortable with the implied association with the upper classes but had to bear in mind that to Rose, anything a step up from a mattress in a shop doorway was probably defined as 'classy'. A life on the streets is not compliant with personal hygiene, and in contrast to a bleached-clean kitchen we both smelt of damp, rotten rags that have spent the last two months neglected at the back of the shed, far removed from the exciting home-improvement projects that may or may not be planned in the next two to three years.

I suggested that Rose have a bath to try and shed some of the layers of dirt that were deeply ingrained into the nooks and crannies of her bony physique. I pointed her in the direction of the bathroom, giving her two newly cleaned, conditioned and folded towels. I sanctioned the use of my Radox Woodland Glade bubble bath, while warding her away from tampering with Nancy's toiletry products. Not wishing to be overbearing, I returned to the ground floor and awarded myself a wee lie-down on the sofa. I gazed out through the conservatory into the garden and watched as a small, unidentifiable bird nibbled at the feeder. Blissfully unaware of the contradictions of human existence, the bird was content to feast on the bountiful seed handily packed in a plastic funnel for its delectation. I looked on in awe and wished I was drifting in the thermals, up, up and away into the bright blue sky.

I was woken from my brief, unplanned power nap by my dear Nancy, who'd shaken me back into life. Her beautiful brown eyes were framed within her horn-rimmed specs; her luscious greying locks sat comfortably upon her well-proportioned shoulders. Comrades, I can confirm that absence does make the heart grow fonder. The last time I'd spent two nights away from home was for the Sustainable Housing Conference, Manchester, 1999. While I have no problem with the North, their dietary overreliance on gravy and chips played havoc with my digestive system. As northerners would say, I got right bunged up, and rather than attending a series of seminars on environmental-planning law, I spent the afternoon of day three of the conference residing on the hotel toilet.

Nancy's relief that I had returned unscathed soon turned to anger. She was not appreciative of my decision to go off grid, leaving her to worry if I was lying dead in a ditch somewhere. She'd had to endure a police interrogation and fend off the unrelenting gossiping tongues of Burhampton. She said that she had felt 'abandoned and under siege'.

As my leadership team takes shape, I must remember not to allocate public liaison and communication responsibilities to Nancy. She is far too kind, caring and considerate to deal with the right-wing propaganda machine that would drag her through its sordid cogs and wheels. The police had been asking about my whereabouts but, as far as I can tell, were not looking to press charges. However, the American coffee scumbags had been in touch, demanding that I reimburse the cost of the stolen coffees. The tax-dodging bastards have got a cheek. Nancy had paid on my behalf with no questions asked. I felt disappointed that she hadn't resisted their corporate might but felt that it wasn't the right time to pull her up on her behaviour.

I tried to paper over the cracks that had inevitably opened in my absence, by rising from the finely engineered comfort of the floral-patterned three-seater sofa, purchased by Nancy during one of her home-furnishing expeditions, and embarked on a consolatory hug. The hug was cautiously accepted, but I was advised to soak in the bath and decontaminate before any future contact was made.

At this moment, Nancy heard the undisguisable sounds of human feet walking along the upstairs landing.

My unique blend of visionary thinking mixed with a healthy dose of pragmatic realism was absent as I tried to think of a quick fix to the approaching three-way standoff. Eastwood, Van Cleef and the Mexican chap, sun beating down, eyes squinting, I eyed the socialist treasure trove that stood between us and sought inspiration from the enchanting sounds of Ennio Morricone. While Eastwood was a signed-up Republican, he did know how to deal with high-pressure situations. He was a man of a few well-placed words that would cut through the tension. In many of his roles this was then followed by shooting someone, except when flexing his underrated comedy muscles in *Every Which Way but Loose*, with my all-time favourite performing monkey, Clyde. There are differing opinions of the ethics of forcing animals into the Hollywood spotlight. I'm sure Clyde was provided with an endless supply of bananas and, being free of the laws of the jungle, lived a life of comfort. Of course, as is often the case when you peer behind the veneer of the big screen, there may have been a life of exploitation, neglect and sadness. At some point, I'd pluck up the courage to view his Wikipedia page and run the risk of having my rose-tinted view of simian thespianism shattered into a thousand tiny pieces. A harsh price to pay for subverting evolution for the sake of some mint classic laughs. Clyde, if you suffered for your art, let me tell you, it was bloody well worth it. With his disdain for authority and his well-timed slapstick humour, I think he would have made an excellent foil to Bobby's diligence, loyalty and occasional bad moods. If the wee black-furred fella was feeling a bit low, Clyde would find a way to elicit a belly laugh that would lighten the mood.

Rose, unaware of Nancy's presence, came dancing into the living room, bedecked in a towel, singing 'It's Raining Men' by the Weather Girls.

She wailed with delight and shimmied to the imaginary beat.

As she probably hadn't had a hot bath for months, if not years, no wonder she had entered a state of bubble bath-soaked euphoria. I have on occasion reached a Radox Woodland Glade-induced high – its finely perfumed suds flowing through my nasal passages straight into my outer cortex. Hats off to their legion of liquid soap alchemists. Whatever they put in their bottles, it has been refined over the years to what can only be described as sensorial perfection.

In our several decades together, I've rarely seen Nancy lost for words, but this was one of those occasions.

Rose, still rushing on her post-bath high, was happy to fill the void, and introduced herself as 'Rose, straight from the motherfucking streets of Weyford'.

Nancy replied that she was, 'Nancy from, erm, Burhampton, previously residing in Essex and born and brought up in Gloucestershire.'

She left out any profanity to her geographic-based introduction. Swearing just wasn't part of Nancy's DNA. She would tolerate my use of the second-tier swears, which I used when necessary to accentuate some of my opinions. When the opportunity arose, I would slip in a bloody, a tits or, when pushing my luck, a shit.

As Nancy reached out and tentatively shook Rose's freshly cleansed hands, I took the opportunity to interject

83

with a condensed debrief of the last couple of days' activities. Nerves were getting the better of me, and certain details were lost in translation. Nancy listened patiently as I rambled my way through a potted history of recent events. Rose filled in the occasional missing detail. For someone with a brain addled with booze, she had a remarkably good memory. In her recollections she was, unfairly in my opinion, highly critical of Fairness Man and his direct approach to social intervention.

I was expecting Nancy, and her underlying ethics of care, benevolence and forgiveness, to come to Fairness Man's defence, but I was sorely wrong. She said that my new alter ego had 'created nothing but trouble' and was an 'undeniable pain in the neck'.

I stepped away from the harsh glare of shared antipathy for Fairness Man and took the opportunity to launch Rose's structured metaphysical reintegration programme into the air with a full twisted double pike before landing, knees flexed, into the well-padded gym mat of matrimony. Nancy seemed conflicted. While her good nature wanted to provide and care for others, housing a stranger pushed beyond the bounds of what she considered her social responsibility. I explained that Rose would be happy to reside in the shed and would require little else beyond some basic food stuffs and a daily supply of alcohol, which I would seek to gently reduce over time, easing its addictive hold over mind and body.

Rose said it would be, 'Fucking magic, Mrs Barry. I'll be out of your hair in a few days, once I get my shit together.'

I explained to Rose that even the most able student would need more than a few days to reach the higher planes of social awareness and physical harmony, even if she decided not to take the optional integrated lifestyle module that I had been mulling over.

Nancy, with characteristic grace, seemed to accept the situation, while casting me a look which meant there's more to be said on this matter, once we are alone. Rather than wait for a firm agreement to the shed-centric housing solution, I pressed on and suggested Rose get dressed in the spare room, while I prepared the camp bed. With Rose out of earshot, Nancy was able to express the full breadth of her feelings. I hadn't quite prepared myself for what could be described as the type of primal screaming exercise favoured by LSD-experimenting 1960s psychotherapists. She shifted from a high-pitched wail that moved through the octaves into a guttural growl, not dissimilar from Barry White in his love walrus heyday. After our many years of marriage, this was the first time I'd experienced the full range of her vocal register. Even in this state of high emotion, Nancy didn't stoop to bad language. I don't even think the Queen could maintain this level of lexical integrity. I'm sure she has her off days, where she refers to her loyal servants as a bunch of wretched pleb fuckwits. Worn down by the monotonous, smile, wave, shake and repeat, her view of humanity slowly sinking into the quicksand that she perused from the lofty heights of her super-privileged malaise. On some levels I agreed with Nancy's critique of my short-term strategic direction. She was right to point out that I had no skills, training and expertise in counselling and supporting the homeless, but what I lacked in this territory, I made up for with my dynamic radicalism. I could already see the positive impact I was having on Rose's spiritual demeanour.

It was if she was edging slowly to a state of wellbeing by observing a man applying his craft with precision.

I was less in agreement when Nancy stated that, 'I'm worried about you, George. It feels like you are rapidly losing touch with reality.'

This cut me to the core. I was trying to forge a new reality, not lose touch with it. I'd have to accept that by challenging the illusionary constructs that people clung to, in order to give them some sense of identity in the atomised consumerist purgatory in which they existed, I was going to be mislabelled an old-fashioned nut job. Eventually you'll see, my dear, that it all makes sense, but until then I would have to be deceptive, play her game, executing my plans in an inconspicuous, incremental phased roll-out. This would be hard with Fairness Man's new-found fame, but like a great artist reinventing themselves, it was achievable. Like Bowie, I would retreat to the industrial bowels of Berlin and create a new, darker, harder version of my vision. An obtuse, intellectual form that would pulse with the steady rhythm of emancipation.

My well-placed offer of a hot brew seemed to ease the obvious tension that had been generated from my dramatic and unannounced re-emergence into the peaceful and uneventful domesticity of Barry Towers.

Nancy's anger subsiding, she agreed that, 'Rose can stay for one night, but then you'll find her a more suitable place to stay. There are charities and hostels that can look after her.'

'Well, where are these charities and hostels now?' I felt like saying, but instead nodded, trying to muster my full placatory energies to neutralise the situation.

Rose returned, giving off the smell of Radox Woodland Glade combined with the stench of clothes that had not seen a sniff of Fairy non-bio tablets, or their inferior own-label bed fellows, for several weeks. Nancy offered to clean her clothes, and Rose gave her a big hug. 'Thanks, you're an angel.'

Nancy smiled, but I could tell she was doing her best to override her nurturing instincts, not wanting to form a bond with Rose that would then have to be broken just as it flourished. 'It's no bother, Rose, no bother at all,' she said, as she went to get some clean clothes for Rose to change into.

I showed Rose to the shed, making a detour past the drinks cabinet and taking a bottle of Dubonnet. I handed it to Rose, who studied its label and, seeing it was 14.8% proof, was satisfied. I know that Betty Ford would frown on my approach, but times have changed, Betty, and you'd better move with them or face extinction. Rose seemed pleased with her new living quarters. With electric fan heater, finely curated toolbox, armchair and an assortment of Southend match programmes to leaf through, there was plenty to keep her entertained. I made up her camp bed, and in came Bobby, jumping up on the cosy duvet laid on top. Bless you, my dear furry friend, you know how to make someone feel at home. I left Rose to settle into her new temporary home and dipped my toe back into Burhampton Forum's tepid waters, where its pond life swam through the green slime of their opinionated algae.

There freshly typed and posted by TonyBeermeister (Tony, the fat, bald publican of The Fox and Hounds), was the topic '*Captain Cappuccino Rides Into Town with Mystery Lady*'. Tony, after your many years imbibing tabloid headlines, I thought you could do better than that. He gave a biased recap of his encounter with Rose and me.

'Captain Cappuccino (better known to you and me as George Barry) visited The Fox and Hounds (winner of the bronze medal in the Surrey Independent Pub awards, guest ales category) with a psycho freak witch who soaked me in a pint of my own beer (Larton Golden Shrew, at an excellent £4.20 a pint) before attacking elderly hero Jack Weir. If you see them, be warned. Let's put the Great back in Britain and stamp out their perverted behaviour.'

The usual suspects chipped in with their inane and misinformed bile. No surprises that RevRightOn was at the front of the queue. Does the modern clergyman spend every waking hour with his eyes glued to a computer screen? If Jesus could see how things had turned out I don't think he would have made the effort. His theory was that Rose and I had *'been radicalised by an Islamic Splinter Group hellbent on undermining the wonder of Anglo-Christian beliefs and values'.* He was confident that through an aggressive form of religious reprogramming he could *'decontaminate our minds and return Burhampton to its natural order'.*

At this point Wilko (Chinny) entered the discussion. He believed that, *'There must be some sort of external influence. Barry seems like a simple man who likes simple pleasures. While a tad eccentric, I'm sure he means nobody any harm.'*

He stated that he was *'on good terms with the old chap. I shall pay him a visit and get to the bottom of this'.*

Oh, shitting hell, the last thing I needed was that ample-jawboned historic military fanatic invading my personal space.

Simmonds53 piped up from his gold-plated bunker, *'That makes jolly good sense. I shall leave it in your capable hands.'* He went on to give an update on The Golden Tandoori, saying that *'a decision would be imminent'.* Through his contacts in the council he felt extremely confident that *'the right decision would be made'.*

The smug idiot. While my area of expertise is in the administrative aspects of local housing policy, I need to find a way to shuffle sideways into the world of environmental regulations. Not wishing to have too many plates spinning at once, I made a quick decision to get Rose bedded into her reintegration programme before doubling down on my efforts to sustain the cuisine of the sub-continent. Fighting battles on too many fronts had been the undoing of many a great leader. I would learn from the past and be single-minded on the path to a new society. But I had to act fast. The days of the five-year plans are over, my friends. There would be no protracted industrial targets and Stakhanovite ideals. While the thought of the Swine humping salt in the Urals gave me a moment of misanthropic joy, it was not from the darker side of humanity that I will plough my field. The flowers of socialism will grow from the seeds of compassion. My plans would work on shorter cycles of five minutes, five days or, if absolutely necessary, five weeks. This is where the influence of Fairness Man came to bear, firing up a high-octane, instinctive way of working.

Resisting the urge to enter the forum discussion, and not wanting to waste a single key stroke on the Spatchcock imbeciles, I turned my efforts inwards, switched my laptop off and went to enquire on the established (Nancy) and newly acquainted (Rose) members of the household. To my surprise they were busy in the kitchen, chatting away as if old friends and preparing a sponge cake for the arrival of Sophie and Nathan. It transpires that Rose had been a trained pastry chef before her life spiralled into an abyss, until that fateful moment when Fairness Man scooped her up from the gutter. While I'm able to cater for the savoury end of the culinary spectrum, baking was not an area I had explored. It was the endless measuring that put me off. The rigid rules and methods of the cake overlords conflicted with the nutritional alchemic approach I favoured, when put to the task of whipping up a fine bacon sandwich or preparing a delicious plate of bangers and mash. Rose and Nancy gave me a cursory glance before their eyes returned to mixing bowl and the oven. I was happy to step aside and pray that a friendship would blossom that could help extend Rose's stay beyond the sanctioned twenty-four hours. I took my cue to leave, giving me the chance to run a steaming hot bath and wash away the grime of my life as a homeless missionary. I lay back and let the Radox Woodland Glade suds soak deep into my skin. The sud level was suboptimal due to Rose's liberal use of the fragranced bubble bath fluid, having only left the residue of its chemical magic in the bottle, but high enough to not distract from my bathing rituals.

Sophie and Nathan arrived and were in good spirits. Their youthful enthusiasm and obsession with popular culture provided a welcome contrast to my relentless intellectual brilliance. They were a bit thrown by Rose's presence, but by constructing an explanation based on an imagined format for a reality programme, they seemed to except her presence as being quite normal. I called the format *Homeless House Invasion*. Just sit back and enjoy the tension, the laughs, the tears, as two worlds collide.

How will a homeless person survive when catapulted into Middle England? How will their hosts cope with their new guest? I considered adding a dating angle or possibly a talent contest, as they seem to be wedged into most popular TV these days, but I could see I'd already gained Sophie and Nathan's attention and an additional element to the format was unnecessary.

Nathan was, 'Well stoked. This is like some, kinda, real-life TV experience. I'm so going to put this on my Instagram. Boom.' Like a political Pied Piper I was playing my tune and he was nestling unknowingly into my socialist bosom.

Sophie was also positive towards my endeavours. I think she is starting to see me in a new light. A man who in his retirement is straddling the generational divide and connecting with the youth zeitgeist. She loved my 'coffee guy idea': 'There are some great memes of you out there. The girls at work think you're so cool.'

Nathan said he'd 'love to have as many views as me'. It turns out that the film of Fairness Man swiping the caffeinated beverages had been watched over 34,000 times on YouTube, whereas Nathan's workout videos are only getting on average eighty-five people viewing them. Well, Nathan, young lad, you need a calling that connects with the nation, and you're not going to achieve that through your mind-numbing exercise regime. I was disappointed that Sophie and Nathan had failed to understand the significance and symbolism of Fairness Man's actions, but at least I'd got their generation's attention.

I quizzed them both on what I should do next, or more specifically, 'How can I connect with their mindset and mobilise action?'

Sophie suggested a line of merch (that's merchandise to you and me), such as hoodies, T-shirts and the like, as 'all the influencers do it'.

Yes, dear comrades, I'm an influencer now. I was conflicted that by creating an elegant yet sophisticated line of quality merchandise for the discerning young, I would be contributing to the environmental impact of fast fashion, while simultaneously filling the coffers of the George Barry revolutionary treasure trove.

Sophie's next idea felt both achievable but free of the strains of capitalist hypocrisy. She recommended I choreograph a dance routine, something that people could easily copy, film and share, ad nauseam. I mulled this over and decided if I could combine a dance routine with some performance poetry, I could both entertain and enlighten my growing audience.

Sophie and Nathan's attempts at conversation with Rose were less fruitful. They put themselves to the task of being an imaginary reality TV couple but struggled to find any common ground with their allocated Homeless House Invader. Rose had never been to a gym, used Instagram, heard of kale or embarked on an eight-week flexitarian detox diet.

Even Rose's baking prowess was unable to provide common ground for them to bond. Yes, you would have thought the age-old blend of eggs, flour, butter, sugar and optional icing, would have provided a safe haven in which all humanity could take shelter. But, I'm sorry to announce, comrades, that even the realm of the humble cake has gone to cock. When the offering of a slice of Battenberg doesn't build bridges, no wonder we are faced with the inevitable collapse of civilisation as we know it.

Nathan said, 'I can't eat cake as it's not part of my high-protein diet and will threaten the definition of my abs and potentially my glutes.'

This prompted Rose to ask, 'What the fucking hell are you talking about? It's just sponge cake, you muppet.'

Nathan didn't know how to respond, as I imagine he surrounds himself with likeminded PE obsessives who worship protein, abs and glutes like the Mayans worshipped the sun.

Nancy broke the awkward silence that followed by announcing, in the style of a highly experienced yet overbearing events coordinator, that we would reconvene for dinner at 19:00, giving us all two hours' free time in which to relax. Rose took the opportunity to retreat to the shed. Nancy and Sophie decided to use their allocated free time to have a glass of fizz and catch up on the latest gossip. This left Nathan staring and swiping his phone at pictures of lycra-clad men and women in various states of discomfort. It was a readily available visual morphine that locked him in an agitated trance.

I, ever-productive, seized on the luxury of 120 fantastic minutes, there in front of me like beautiful capsules of time ready to be utilised. Yes, I would give Rose an introductory tutorial on rehabilitation and resilience techniques in response to neo-liberal consumerism. I hadn't written any notes but was happy to extemporise rather than leave Rose in psychological purgatory for any longer. As I walked up the garden path, I felt the tingle of positive energy spread from my toes up to my ears and I felt compelled to give a solo acapella rendition of 'September' by Earth, Wind and Fire, where I switched from the standard lyrical pattern by interjecting a classic 'doo-wop' motif favoured by many a vocal ensemble and the odd 'boom, boom' of a bass drum, to add an extra layer of musical depth. It may have been my imagination, but I'm sure some sort of wild fowl joined in and added a beautiful chirping melody. Nature was plopping a sumptuous auditory cherry on top of my innovative reworking of the feel-good soul classic.

My upbeat mood came to a halt when I got to the shed and found that Rose had disappeared. On the floor I spotted the tell-tale sign of a discarded Dubonnet bottle top. I feared that in a knee-jerk reaction to Sophie and Nathan's unsuccessful attempts at verbal exchanges, that the pilot episode of *Homeless Home Invasion* had been a ratings flop. I took it as a personal compliment that I was unable to master the basics of mass-market TV. It was a welcome ink blot to my mostly high-achieving school report. OK, I struggled in maths, and the sciences let me down, but I excelled in the fact-laden terrain of history. God bless Mr Perkins and his humorous re-enactments of the siege of Berlin and Hitler's suicide, lurching out of the bunker with exaggerated goose step, cod German accent and false moustache. Teaching gold like that would never make it in today's educational straight jacket, otherwise known as the national curriculum. A system that churned out a yearly batch of institutionalised automatons. Time permitting, I will develop a new school syllabus built on the three pillars of visionary thinking, mindfulness and reconstructing social norms. I would use Fairness Man sparingly for PE lessons and extra-curricular educational trips. I think he could be a hit with the infant demographic, imbuing them with our socialist credo through the joy of outdoor pursuits.

I looked for further clues to Rose's whereabouts and saw that the gate to the side passage was open. I needed to find her quickly and shield her from the various predatory characters of Burhampton, who live in fear of their peaceful idyll being contaminated by external influences. I broke into a canter, and once my legs were bedded in, started to gallop to the high street. As most of the Burhampton residents abhor the idea of being a pedestrian, the pavements lay empty, providing a clear path for me to make fast progress.

On reaching the high street, my eyes scanned past the shop fronts of Tesco Express, Atkins Butchers, Burhampton Bakers, the American coffee-shop chain, whose name will not pass my lips, and The Weeping Willows gift shop, before spotting the unwitting prey sitting on the floor outside the post office, talking with Reverend Ormerod. Bloody typical that it's probably the only time this week that he's managed to drag himself away from the Burhampton Forum to fetch some essential supplies, before retreating to his cocoon of self-serving theology, and he bumps into Rose.

I bade the Reverend good day and he replied in a manner that was complimentary and patronising in equal parts: 'This young lady tells me you've been playing the good Samaritan, George Barry. Full of surprises, aren't you? Glad to see you have strong Christian values. After the coffee incident, I was concerned that those ISIS chaps had infected your mind, so to speak. Lot of it about. Radicalisation, I think they call it.'

On another occasion, I would love to have instigated a theological debate encompassing my atheism, while carefully unpicking and undermining his Islamic prejudice, but there was the more pressing concern of assisting Rose's safe return to Barry Towers.

Rose was making good progress through the Dubonnet. 'Tastes like shit, but does the fucking trick,' was her verdict on the French aperitif. 'I'm better on the streets, not causing you any bother,' she added.

While I admired her selfless attitude, I was not going to abandon her. Reverend Ormerod admitted that he had no experience in the area of homelessness but was sure there were organisations that could help, and he was willing to spend an hour or two doing some internet research to see what comes up.

'Do pop into the church if you feel like repenting any sins. That is a service we offer to all and at no cost,' he said.

And they wonder why the church doesn't play the part in society that it once did, strewth. I settled the Reverend's concerns by stating that I had no contact with any ISIS members and that I would seek to find a permanent residence for Rose. This seemed to satisfy the nosy do-gooder, but let's see what he types up on the Burhampton Forum, the duplicitous bastard.

With the Reverend out of the way I managed to coax Rose to her unsteady feet. 'You're a good man, George, but when you put on that mask you start acting like a tit.' Poor Fairness Man, misunderstood and castigated at every turn. In the dance I construct to build his internet fame, I must find ways to bust some of the fake news that surround his enigmatic personality.

Rose's arm resting over my shoulder, we ambled back home. Approaching Barry Towers, I could see that Chinny Wilkinson was on the doorstep chatting to Nancy, his extended jaw reflecting the glare of the early evening sun. Everywhere I turn I'm hounded. Can't they just leave me alone to lead a radical yet kind-hearted revolution unconstrained by their intrusions? I told Rose that we should lay low and hide behind a nearby tree, but in her intoxicated state I think what she heard was, why don't you reprise your rendition of 'It's Raining Men' so that the neighbours can enjoy the flowing melodies and gentle cadence of your angelic voice? Chinny's ears quickly tuned into the high-energy disco classic, triggering memories of latent homosexual rites of passage from his days as flanker in the school's second fifteen rugby team. His head pivoted, he fixed his eyes on us both, smiled and let off a bellowing, 'Barry, you wild card, you. I think we need to talk.'

I could tell that Rose had taken an instant disliking to Chinny, rooted in an evolutionary survival response to long-faced male strangers with a questionable dress sense and a penchant for historic military strategies. Even though the nearest he'd probably got to a military strategy was playing Battleships (I imagine he would be intimidated by the more complex gameplay of Risk). 'Who is this posh dick?' was Rose's opening gambit.

I billed Chinny as a harmless busybody, filtering out the malevolent side to him and his fellow Spatchcock conspirators, as I didn't want Rose to feel perturbed, potentially side-tracking her rehabilitative journey. Needless to say, this psychological manipulative technique proved fruitless in diffusing the tension between what you would describe as a clash of personalities.

Chinny bowled up, chest puffed, eyes twitching, bellowing like Brian Blessed on high-grade amphetamines, and introduced himself and his intentions.

He was concerned that our 'behaviour was straying into the anti-social and it pains me to say, un-British, dear chap and chapess'.

He referred to my coffee-redistribution episode and put Rose on the spot regarding her altercation with Tony.

Rose made her views clear that Tony was 'a complete fuck head who needed to be put in his place. Fuck him and his fucking little pub'.

Things escalated as Chinny used the irksome phrase, 'Do you know who I am?', to which she replied, 'Yes, the prime minister of go fuck yourself.'

This was a verbal salvo that knocked off his well-meaning mask to expose the repulsive reality.

'Barry, you and your tart are playing with fire, mate. You aren't going to get in the way of us making Great Britain great again. Do you hear me?' he said, as he stormed off, ready to rally the Spatchcock troops into battle.

Like all master tacticians, I knew that Fairness Man was needed to mount a rapid response to stay one step ahead of the impending Spatchcockian attack. While he hadn't won over the trust of Rose and Nancy to date, this was a chance to build bridges with Barry Towers while simultaneously leveraging his social-media footprint via the medium of dance to reconnect with the wider world.

I safely returned Rose to her camp bed and recommended that she have a well-deserved rest following her recent altercation. She jumped at the chance and moved swiftly into a comatose state. Sprinting fast, to avoid detection and unnecessary conversation, I made my way past the kitchen, where Nancy and Sophie were making the finishing touches to dinner. In our bedroom, I rifled out the mask, cape and neckerchief from my backpack. Making a quick change, Fairness Man bounded down the stairs, where he was greeted by Nathan. He requested a selfie, which was duly excepted, on the proviso that it was instantly shot into the digital ether.

Fairness Man asked Nathan to set the camera running, before breaking into an unrehearsed dance routine. I had to think fast and pull a series of moves straight from the George Barry archives. The archives were pretty lean, but there was a small supply of rhythmic shapes lurking in a folder marked Ritzy's Soul Classics, 1983–85. I opened the folder and the youthful moves of a man expressing his inner turmoil and desires came forth. Shoulder drop, into side shuffle, head nod and repeat, that's how to work it, baby. Fairness Man instructed Nathan to lay down some rudimentary beat box. Through a combination of nerves and inexperience his delivery was lacking, with the bass drum sounding a bit more like a playground raspberry. He did not let Nathan's lack of technique hold him back and shifted seamlessly between moves before attempting some freestyle poetry. Unfortunately, there were no poetic archives to exploit but Fairness Man had a natural flare for ad-lib rhyming and lyrical word play.

I'm a masked crusader bringing you justice
Burning down inherently prejudiced and elitist institutions
*   with a recently purchased box of safety matches*
Some say I'm causing trouble or perhaps I'm a bit annoying
*   due to my overenthusiasm*
But all I'm trying to do is redistribute wealth from those
*   who have, to those who don't have 'em*
These Make Great Britain Great people are a bunch of shits
To put it bluntly they're getting on my tits

Fairness Man had no idea or even cared if that was a haiku or sonnet; he'd nailed his ethos in a ten- to twenty-second video. He got a confirmatory nod from Nathan that it was in the can and thanked him for his assistance. The young man looked on in wonder and imagined what life would be like if he had the same mental and physical ability. Once I have the time, I'll craft a mindfulness programme for Nathan, and many people like him, so they are inspired to act, without losing confidence due to their obvious lack of talent.

Fairness Man made a quick exit to the front door as he spied Nancy approaching using his twenty-twenty peripheral vision. There was no time to chat and no time to enjoy a tasty home-cooked dinner; these are the sacrifices that great change is built on. As he sprinted down the road he soon regretted having not mounted the trusty Raleigh. Despite his athletic ability and prime physique, he'd managed to strain his right hip during his triumphant poetic dance piece of, dare I say it, accessible yet avant-garde artistic communication. He slowed down to an energetic walk and prepared himself to enter the hornet's nest. He needed to divide and conquer the Spatchcock stronghold, through the most divisive and deluded dominion of all, religion. Yes, he could shatter the antiquated iconography of the Anglican church, realigning its purpose and using its instruments of mind control to wrong-foot the Spatchcockers and build the growing momentum for change.

Fairness Man set his navigational compass in the direction to St Mary's Church. Feeling continued discomfort in his hip, his pace slowed further to a standard pedestrian stroll as he reached the high street. The residents of Burhampton looked on in awe as he passed them by. His superpowers emanating from every pore, piercing through their humdrum routines. There was a laugh here and there, and the occasional coffee-related heckle, but this was part and parcel of being a celebrity activist. If he had to entertain in order to educate, then so be it, it was, unfortunately, the modern way.

Fairness Man reached the entrance to St Mary's Church and paused. He breathed deep into his nostrils, preparing to put his scientifically grounded atheism on pause, and radically remould religion in the British Isles to a degree not witnessed since Henry VIII. He entered the church and was met with the mournful eyes of Jesus looking down on him from the cross. Two icons connected through shared persecution, a yearning for a better world and a taste for wine of all denominations, except rosé. The church was empty, with Reverend Ormerod most probably tap, tap tapping his bigoted views to his receptive cyber audience. Fairness Man walked down the aisle and circumnavigating what he understood to be the biblical stage, he found a wooden door. It was dark and uninviting, warding people off the murky inner sanctum of the church. It took more than a spooky door to ward off someone of Fairness Man's stature. He marched straight through into battle, conjuring up the spirit of the crusades, minus the belief in Christ and the vehement anti-Muslim agenda.

The room contained a variety of religious paraphernalia. There were Bibles stacked in neat piles. The tomes of mind control: dusty, neglected and anachronistic, like the men who peddled its commands, feathering their privileged theological nests, rife with righteousness and moral superiority. In the far corner was a tea urn and a biscuit tin. It was through the humble brew, complemented by a dunked digestive or rich tea, that many men of the cloth had syphoned money from the old and infirm. At the end of the room was a clothes rail, a couple of metres long. Hanging from it was an array of religious robes of different sizes and colours. To Fairness Man's untrained eye, the significance of the different garments was lost on him, but he knew an opportunity when he saw one. Running his hands through the robes, they settled on the traditional black cassock and white dog collar. They were a perfect accompaniment to his cape and mask.

He put on the cassock and, while not designed for high-adrenaline exercise, it added a layer of dignity to his image. He decided to keep wearing the red neckerchief, concealing the dog collar and a reminder that he did things his own way and wasn't going to be dragged down into the dogmatic religious cesspool. He was going to reinvent religion from its core – shake it up and bring it in line with his views and aims.

His first decision was to get rid of God, or at least put him, her, they or it to the sidelines. Yes, God was out and so was, sorry to say, Jesus and his disciples. He knew that this wouldn't be to the tastes of many of the current Christian fraternity, but the more progressive end of the spectrum would come on board. One aspect of the Bible he was happy to co-opt and modernise was the good old Ten Commandments. He had to admit many of the commandments still rung true, except perhaps the bit about coveting your neighbour's ox. But let's face it, the commandments were pretty much common sense and lacked any degree of inspiration and imagination. You did feel that if God did exist, he, she, they or it, was a Steady

Eddie type. Someone who was happy to take the middle ground and not upset the apple cart. A bit like the Liberal Democrat party, nice but lacking depth. Like Moses on mount something or another, Fairness Man needed to rise above the populous of Burhampton and proclaim his beliefs upon the fragmented, myopic flock.

As Fairness Man basked in his new-born Christianity, he let the love of an absent God flow over him, when his bat-like hearing picked up the approaching feet of the Reverend. This was his cue to head yonder and spread the good word.

While a brilliant big-picture thinker, Fairness Man did struggle with his short-term memory. With so many great ideas flooding through his various lobes, it was no wonder that some of the more prosaic aspects of daily life removed themselves from his mind. What he failed to remember, as he attempted to emulate Seb Coe's 1,500-metre Olympic Gold in Moscow – cruelly smiting his asthmatic foe, Steve Ovett, which launched Coe's smug bonce onto the unwitting British public for the subsequent decades – was that his right hip was not fully functioning, only allowing a top speed of approximately eight to nine miles an hour. Under normal conditions, fetching the milk, going to the toilet, this would be fine, but Fairness Man didn't operate under anything you would describe as normal.

Before he managed to make his way through the wooden door, Reverend Ormerod had caught up, firing off pious venom.

'Jesus Christ, Barry, what the bloody hell are you doing, man? Take off those holy garments at once or I shall be forced to report you to the Archbishop of Canterbury. And you don't want his holy wrath taking vengeance on your crazy ass.'

Fairness Man explained that, 'I am operating within an entirely different belief system than the Archbishop, and it is nothing to be concerned about. I'm approaching Christianity from a new angle that I don't think either of you would be able to sufficiently grasp at this juncture.'

Reverend Ormerod offered me, George Barry, help and guidance, 'To pull you out of the heretical hole in which you have descended, weighed down by your sins and heathen beliefs.'

Fairness Man reassured the Reverend that George was, 'In fine fettle and that as a matter of urgency I must leave. Toodle-oo.'

As Fairness Man walked away, the Reverend jumped to the floor and grabbed him by the ankles.

'Those robes are my lifeblood; without them I'm nothing. Thirty-five years, Barry, I've been serving the good people of Burhampton, and you come and snatch it all away. Have you no shame?'

In different circumstances, I would have imparted some mindfulness techniques to help the Reverend overcome the separation anxiety he was suffering from. The years of indoctrination and dogma had taken their toll. Living on his own, mind free to develop deluded conspiracy theories fuelled by likeminded religious cyber nutters. It was a recipe for disaster.

With the Reverend wrapped around his ankles, but the pressing need to communicate to the citizens of Burhampton and set their minds free from their ideological prison, Fairness Man was faced with a dilemma. He was a pacifist and did not condone physical violence against vulnerable individuals. However, leafing through the small print of his values and ethics, he dug up an interesting sub-principle that he was able to put into play. Limited grappling was allowed in emergency situations as long as no severe or lasting physical pain was inflicted. Due to his impeded bipedal velocity, he needed to use lateral thinking to find a way out of his predicament. He unclasped the sweaty limpet hands of the Reverend and found cover behind the religious robes hanging from the clothes rail. They provided a musty barrier, shielding him from the volatile preacher. Fairness Man only had a few seconds' respite before the barrier was breached. The Reverend surged forward and into the robes to apprehend his foe, tripping over the steel rod that run along the bottom of the clothes rail. This sent him clattering head-first into the sturdy walls of the inner sanctum, rendering him unconscious. As Fairness Man observed the crumpled clergyman, a ray of light streamed through a window onto the crown of our masked hero's head, anointing him and his new-founded credo. The old guard had been cast aside and he was free to walk on, albeit with the need for some ibuprofen, and open a new chapter unconstrained by fable, patriarchy and blatant homophobia. Fairness Man ventured out of the church and into the community, feeling the weight of history dissolve behind him.

Fairness Man was now accustomed to people's stares, mutterings and poorly disguised guffaws. He accepted it as part of his soundtrack: the bass drum, hi-hat and snare, providing a steady rhythm over which the strings of social change could eddy and flow into a confluence of radical thoughts, inverting power structures and generating the hydro-electric wattage to light up the minds of all he encountered. Soaking up the sweet music, he broke into a groovy shuffle, strictly four beats to the bar, at his preferred 120 beats-per-minute tempo. He reached the high street and considered what he should mount to get a suitable vantage point to address his people. His hawk-like eyes pinpointed some newly erected scaffolding that covered the facade of Watnams Bookmakers. The scaffold had been erected by Rodney Bowes, who, on his advertising placard, proudly proclaimed that, 'He always gets it up, leaving every customer satisfied.' While Fairness Man paid no heed to innuendo-laden promotional by-lines, he was reassured that they appeared to be a well-respected outfit.

As Fairness Man started to scale the scaffolding, Rolly Peterson emerged from the bookies looking sheepish. He is known to like the occasional flutter, but I have good information that his wife is less keen on his mild gambling addiction. I've never met Mrs Jane Peterson but, according to Nancy, she runs Burhampton Tennis Cub social committee with an iron fist. She'd turned down Nancy's suggestion of a summer fete to raise funds for the local school, by replying that, 'Can't the little brats raise their own bloody funds? The lazy shits.'

Poor Rolly, never having the confidence to think for himself, just a scared boy dropped off for another term to face weeks of bullying and ritualistic humiliation: the brutal rites of passage of the establishment. I can help you, poor Rolly, thought Fairness Man, as he stared down on his greasy brown side parting and imagined him spending his cherished fifty-pence pocket money on a iced bun from the school tuck shop, affording a moment of joyous respite before the torment continued. A habit for excessive comfort eating that had lasted a lifetime. As a newly appointed deity, Fairness Man would need disciples, and who better than the weakest Spatchcockian link? With Rolly on board he could destabilise their power base and take control of the local narrative.

'Rolly, hold your step, I have some great words to impart. Something amazing is about to unfold, and I want you to listen.'

Rolly replied with something about 'people being worried about his behaviour' and 'get down from there and let's have a chat', but Fairness Man was not one to be distracted by the idle tittle-tattle of the chatterers and gossipers, who squandered their privilege with their incessant prying into other people's affairs.

Fairness Man reached the second tier of scaffolding and was satisfied that its height, of approximately two and a half metres, would provide the optimum acoustic reach, so that the sleepwalking residents could hear him. He raised his arms outstretched above his head and began.

'Ladies and gentlemen, we salute you and the nation of shopkeepers we once were, revered by Napoleon and the other great European military dictators of his time. Unfortunately, due to the corporate might and the greed of the ruling classes, the foundations of the daily life you take for granted are crumbling. We mourn the sad passing of Wickham's DIY Store – ground down by the tyranny of the big retailers and their vast stock, online ordering and competitive pricing strategies. The Wickhams, you provided a fine service, facilitating those often fiddly small DIY jobs around the home. You will be missed.'

He held an imaginary Phillips screwdriver above his

head, took a pause for breath and saw that his words were already having an impact, as Rolly had been joined by an elderly woman who Fairness Man recognised but didn't know by name.

'Friends, Burhamptonians and country people, the movement has begun. For real change we need to make radical decisions, and with that in mind, I have some big news. God, Jesus, i.e. God's son, and the holy ghost – I'm not sure of the holy ghost's relation to God – have gone. They are extinct, defunct, departed, left, etc., etc. They played their part in anaesthetising your spirit, your gusto, your inner child. They have destroyed your imagination and imposed a soporific morality that strengthens the status quo. The archaic spiritual hole that they leave behind will be filled by me.'

'Look, I know some of you liked the singing, free wine and companionship – that's fine, that stays, I just need to smooth a few things over with Reverend Ormerod first. There will also be a reworking of the commandments – stay tuned on social media channels for that. So, like Jesus, I need the help of the people. My recruitment of disciples starts right now, and I'm pleased to announce that this is your lucky day, Rolly Peterson, you're signed up. You are my Paul, John, Peter, take your pick – you're the chief honcho disciple numero uno. You will feed off my aura and disseminate the good word. Repeat after me, I feel the power, I feel it.'

Rolly Peterson stood alone, as the elderly woman who had joined the throng had obviously struggled to hear Fairness Man clearly, or was perhaps experiencing the onset of dementia, so had walked away. The solitary

Spatchcockian was speechless, as he took in the enormity of the responsibility that had been laid upon him. Fairness Man felt it only right that he use his empathic ability and speak on his behalf.

'Rolly, I know you are overwhelmed with wonder, but come with me, let us eat and drink from the same table. Let us find a path to inclusion that is welcoming of culinary creeds, that supports the little guy, the trampled, the neglected. Let's strive for a different kind of Great Britain, where the spicy onion bhaji sits shoulder to shoulder next to the humble spud. Where a homeless woman is free to admonish the ingrained prejudice of an uneducated publican. Where a man of extraordinary ability is unfettered in his flights of coffee redistribution. Are you in?'

Rolly Peterson, still struggling to take everything in, said, 'Let's go and have a pint and talk things over.'

Fairness Man took this tentative acceptance of his belief system as a victory. I'm sure some of Jesus's early disciples were a bit circumspect with all the humble bragging about healing the sick, turning water to wine and walking on water, but were happy enough to chew the fat about how to get involved with some base-level preaching and charitable acts.

Fairness Man dismounted the scaffolding and embraced his disciple. 'We shall drink from the well of equity, my brother – let us sit together and share our love for the world.'

Rolly, anxiety-ridden with his quiet conformity, repressed feelings and stiff upper lip, found it hard to cope with Fairness Man's alternative outlook and appearance, and requested that he remove his 'ridiculous outfit. You are embarrassing yourself'.

It was hard for Rolly to converse with a fellow man not

sporting, at the bear minimum, some well-ironed slacks and a blazer.

Fairness Man considered Rolly's concerns and, while open to a collaborative relationship with his disciples, told his timid follower to, 'Take the Kool-Aid of a nice, locally brewed pint of frothy ale and dive into a mind-bending world where ideas, theories and dress codes have no boundaries.'

The unlikely partnership made its way down the high street, away from the retail epicentre, towards The Fox and Hounds, which was located on the edge of the central business district, approximately twenty doors down from the post office. As they made this short yet historically significant journey, Fairness Man contemplated an imminent encounter with Tony, in the wake of the recent unresolved altercation with Rose and yours truly. The mildly repellent publican was just the sort of bloody-minded imbecile to hold grudges and let them fester into a ravaging boil of contempt. Fairness Man needed to locate the boil, lance it and let its pus of malcontent drain into the drip tray of negativity. He could then apply the balm of contrition and plant the seed of forgiveness in Tony's subconscious. Where the humble yet intellectual colossus, Mr George Barry, and the troubled, foul-mouthed yet kind-hearted Rose failed, Fairness Man would succeed.

Fairness Man bounded into The Fox and Hounds announcing his presence with a healthy dose of bravado.

'Good day, dear Tony. I make no apologies for my combative collaborators, Mr George Barry and Ms Rose, surname anonymous. They have the right to state their opinions and use necessary verbal and physical force to get their point across when they are confronted with gross ignorance and incompetence, but I'm a man of peaceful intentions and I offer you my politico-spiritual guidance. I'm supported in my aims and service provision by my inaugural disciple, the honourable Mr Rolly Peterson.'

Fairness Man did consider offering Tony a seat at the disciples table but felt he lacked the interpersonal skills needed to uphold and promote the nascent religious doctrine. Tony was a lost sheep who needed to be guided into the pen of democratic harmony. Fairness Man would be the able shepherd, whistling and stick-waving as Rolly, the faithful border collie, barked, slobbered and nudged Tony into a place of happy confinement. Unfortunately, the grotesque landlord hadn't recovered from the events of earlier that day and still had the sight of my good self burnt into his retinas.

'Barry, stop talking bollocks and get out my pub, you're barred.'

Fairness Man felt aggrieved that he was tarred with the same brush as his colleagues and was struggling to create clear water between himself and these mere mortals, excellent as they were, despite the inevitable flaws that are part and parcel of being human. If he had access to the relevant specialist scientific kit, he would hook up Tony to some visual desensitising apparatus and simultaneously bombard him with images of Mr George Barry and Rose, and the beautiful vapours of the essence of freshly picked flora.

'No problem, Tony, I shall be on my way. Before I leave, I ask you to look into your heart and find forgiveness for the exceptionally talented and unconventionally handsome George and Rose, the vociferous and witty raconteur.'

'Piss off, Barry, I've people to serve.'

Oh, Tony, what can we do with lost souls like you?

Fairness Man was unperturbed by the angry publican. He asked his disciple to step outside, where they could make alternative arrangements.

Once free of Tony's idiotic glare, Fairness Man told Rolly that he would use cunning to sneak around into the small yet functional patio beer garden. Its grey slabs of concrete dull and uncared for, like its recalcitrant owner. While this was happening, Rolly would re-enter the pub, purchase two pints, transport them outside, where they could continue their dialogue while enjoying the spring sunshine. What could be easier?

The major stumbling block was Rolly's nervous disposition. Being a freshly appointed disciple and close associate of Fairness Man, had done nothing to overcome his crippling self-doubt. He was worried that Tony would find them out and that he too may face being barred and live in shame, another social outsider forced to drink peacefully in the comfort of his own front room from 3pm onwards, but with special dispensation to start early on the weekend. Fairness Man quelled his concerns by adding in an extra layer of deception that would take our courageous deity undercover. Like Jesus cowering in a dusty cupboard as the Roman army searched the crannies of Judean tenement housing, Fairness Man would hide beneath one of the several beer garden tables. From here he would achieve invisibility, enjoy a refreshing drink, while maintaining audible dialogue by aiming his voice at the two- to three-centimetre gaps between the table-top planks.

Rolly agreed to the plan with one caveat, that he would purchase only one pint, as even the dim-witted Tony would spot the peculiarity of a lone drinker buying two pints. Fairness Man negotiated a G&T as a suitable replacement, as it was passable as an extravagant chaser for a man of Rolly Peterson's status as retired insurance broker and former Spatchcock underling. Meticulous with both numbers and formal dress codes, he was the sort of guy who fitted in and got on with the day's business with a minimum fuss but found the lunch-time pub visit an essential and enjoyable coping mechanism for numbing himself from the grinding tedium of his life.

Fairness Man walked into the beer garden and, on hands and knees, shuffled into place under an empty table in the far corner of the garden. There were only two occupied tables, both engrossed in conversation and not spotting the stealthy crusader. A shifty-looking Rolly appeared, drinks in hand, and, seeing Fairness Man's crouched figure, stepped forth to inaugurate our first supper. Yes, comrades, Rolly had the foresight of also buying two packets of ready-salted crisps, which he had nestled in his armpits, between rib and arm, in that age-old, failsafe carrying technique that most probably dates back to biblical times.

Settling into discussion, I decided it was worthwhile brainstorming a reboot of the Ten Commandments. Rolly still seemed more concerned with my wellbeing, but Fairness Man told him to chill the hell out and get down with some hardcore blue-sky thinking. Rolly, having spent decades following the strict codes of the world of insurance, was being pushed way outside of his extremely limited areas of expertise. Like Jesus, Fairness Man was hoping his disciple would be proactive in driving change, but as Rolly lacked any sense of imagination or purpose, it was inevitable that he would have to spoon-feed him ideas.

Fairness Man started by listing the bankers: the commandments which were common sense and should remain intact. Not murdering, stealing or committing adultery were in; the rest was up for grabs. As fellow animal lovers, they were quick to agree on a new Fourth Commandment: 'Never inflict harm on animals.' On further discussion they ratified a sub-clause allowing animal slaughter for food production. While I was open to living a flexitarian lifestyle and was happy, in principle, to entertain the possibility of veganism, Fairness Man still held on to his carnivorous instincts. He felt that if he was too militant in the application of the Fourth Commandment, it would undermine the burgeoning support and the tireless effort made thus far. Sorry battery-farmed chickens, artificially fattened cows and pigs living in abject misery, your time will come; unfortunately, after legions have been put to death through a brutal electric current, shutting down the operation of their vital organs in a split second. I promise to revise this commandment when the opportunity arises.

Things got more contentious as we moved away from animals into the sticky territory of homo sapiens. Fairness Man suggested the Fifth Commandment be: 'Let the rich pay with a 100% tax on all earnings over £100,000.'

While Rolly was interested in the concept, he quite rightly pointed out that it would be unworkable as high net worth individuals would inevitably use off-shore tax-avoidance schemes and creative accounting techniques to evade paying up. He then went off on a tangent, wanging on about profit incentives, wealth generation and trickle-down effects, at which point Fairness Man had to put his foot down.

'If you are to be a disciple, dear chap, you need to shed the skin of decades of neo-liberal greed in which you have wallowed like a privileged pig, ignorant to human suffering.'

Fairness Man took on board Rolly's feedback and suggested a more ambiguous alternative commandment which could be shaped and used depending on the moment or mood. 'We should all pay our fair share in creating a caring, cooperative society.'

Rolly took issue with the words caring, cooperative, fair and society.

He described it as, 'cloud-cuckoo thinking of daydreamers and scruffy layabouts. The sort of person with questionable facial hair and unschooled in the correct method of ironing a cream cotton chino to accompany a gingham shirt, offset in cooler temperatures by a quilted gilet'.

Fairness Man drew a clear line under their discussions, happy to have buttoned down five solid commandments, albeit with some resistance. With murder, adultery, theft, limited animal rights and the foundations for a fairer, more inclusive society catered for, he was happy to stop for now and complete the remaining commandments on his own, free of the distractions of Rolly's continual interjections and rebuttals. Rolly was more of a critiquer than a collaborator. A man who could be delegated easy tasks but who couldn't be trusted with anything straying into the lands of intellectual endeavour. Fairness Man had overlooked a holistic approach to mental and physical health, the environmental crisis, homelessness, addiction, abuse, immigration, education, and human rights, but I was sure that through my more nuanced and pragmatic approach, we could cover these in the remaining five commandments that were left available. I know, deep down, that people, drained of attention through the constant digital bombardment magnified through the despondent lens of their meaningless lives, devoid of value or purpose, were unlikely to remember anything beyond a three- or four-word slogan.

Rolly finished his pint, as Fairness Man sipped his refreshing house double G&T, ice cubes gently melting into the piquant blend of botanicals, as a wholesome slice of lemon bobbed on top. He dreamt of life in the Raj, a colonial dignitary, drifting down the Ganges on his house boat, before forming a partnership with Gandhi that would lessen Britain's colonial grip on power and pave the road to independence. Rolly, like a stuck record, started his 'George needs help' routine, once again.

Rolly said that he had a 'friend who has trained as a therapist and could help you work through your problems'.

Fairness Man thought this was a bit rich coming from a man who had a bag full of unresolved mental issues, but he humoured him, as he knew Rolly's concerns were a natural outpouring of love from a disciple to their spiritual guide.

Rolly said that he had to get home for a Friday fish supper. The crunch of crispy batter, the warm mush of the pea and the comforting stodge of a chip, washed down with a cold, crisp ale. Oh, how the mundane rituals never cease for mere mortals, even when in the process of shifting the tectonic plates of our existence. Fairness Man thanked Rolly for his unwavering support and his enthusiastic input to the five commandments. He said he would be in touch about next steps and to let him know if anyone else was interested in signing up as a disciple.

Fairness Man felt drained from the day's events and was paying the price for skipping dinner, the ready-salted crisps amplifying his hunger. He was hoping for a portion of food to be sat waiting on the kitchen table, nestled between two plates ready for reheating and consumption, but with three guests residing in Barry Towers, this was unlikely. He finished the G&T and breathed in the remnants of its lemony vapours. Closing his eyes and thinking of calmer times, Test Match Special playing, the breeze blowing through his hair as he drifted off to the sound of the West Indian pace attack at full throttle. A blend of serenity and aggressive sporting combat, the distillation of a perfect summer's day. His bubble of nostalgic tranquillity was shattered by the coarse, bellowing tones of Tony, who was complimenting a custodian on their lovely blouse, an obvious ruse to gawp at her breasts without being pigeonholed as a dirty perv.

Fairness Man needed to extricate himself from the situation pronto, as an unnecessary confrontation with Tony would further drain his ebbing energy. Like all elite athletes and high achievers across different industry sectors, he needed to refuel. He had hoped his new appointment as God would endow him with hidden powers that would override basic physiological needs to eat, urinate, defecate and sleep. To make the Old Testament more palatable, they edited out that on the seventh day God had a lovely fry-up followed by a whopping great shit. With Tony still making a ham-fisted attempt of chatting up the customer with the lovely blouse, Fairness Man rolled from under the table and sprung to his feet. Hip throbbing, he hobbled out of the beer garden and headed towards the safe haven of home.

A few doors down from The Fox and Hounds was The Golden Tandoori, proudly serving the residents of Burhampton since 1995. Fairness Man took the opportunity to enter the curry house and offer his services. He introduced himself to Abdul and offered up his toolkit of skills to help him battle against the scourge of the Spatchcock Society. He reassured Abdul that his new religious dimension was fully compatible with Hinduism and was even thinking of adding one of their gods as a spiritual companion. He asked for his recommendation, on the criteria that they would need to be hardworking, tolerant and with a passion for social regeneration. Abdul explained that he was in fact Muslim and originally from Bangladesh. As Fairness Man got his head around the revelation that the Indian food he cherished wasn't made by Indians, he realised that he would have to use his own spiritual instincts in choosing a suitable Hindu deity that could be fused into his belief system. He had limited knowledge but was aware of the elephant-headed god Ganesha. Their unconventional appearance indicated a tolerant attitude to identity politics that could help in connecting with those alienated by the starchy norms set by the establishment. Having battled against the disadvantage of having an elephant's head to become a god, would show society's outliers that anything is possible. The fusion of ancient Indian spiritualism with brutal revolutionary realism, sat on the reconstructed foundations of Christian morality, had the potential for greatness. Fairness Man revelled in the thought of this smorgasbord of cohabiting faiths, while feeling the pangs of hunger, as he smelt the unmistakable odour of chicken madras.

Abdul, like everyone else, it seemed, raised concerns for my mental wellbeing. 'Mr Barry, are you feeling OK? Would you like a curry?'

Fairness Man explained that George was well catered for and had dinner waiting at home but that he could really do with a couple of poppadoms and some onion bhajis to tide him over. While his delicious appetisers were being prepared, he asked Abdul on the current status of the attempts to shut The Golden Tandoori down based on the alleged un-Britishness of the spicy delights that he prepared daily without fail or complaint.

'These people eat my food for years and now they tell me I'm no good. What is their bloody problem? Now the council environment people have been around, snooping, sniffing and asking questions. I just sell curry, for crying out loud. They tell me there will be a decision within a week. George, I can't take any more of this.'

Fairness Man told Abdul that he and George needed to bed in a homeless reintegration programme over the weekend, while looking to re-establish domestic harmony in Barry Towers, fending off retribution from Reverend Ormerod and the Spatchcockers, while having to evade the strong arm of the law. Once this multi-pronged juggling act had been seen to, he promised that he would pay the Chief Environmental Officer a visit. Unfortunately, this meant a return trip to Weyford, the Sodom or Gomorrah of Surrey, whose residents lay in waiting to be redeemed by Fairness Man and feel his love. There were a considerable percentage of the Weyford population who Fairness Man would rather didn't drink from his holy well of love, but on this point, he had to doff his cap to Jesus and his famous capacity for forgiveness. He would take a leaf out of his book and suck up his anger, prejudice and enmity, and be generous in spirit to some of the most self-serving and atrocious people living within a thirty-mile radius of London.

He wasn't sure where Ganesha would sit on this. Fairness Man listened to his inner voice and, through a spiritual connectiveness technique, tuned into the thoughts of the Elephantine God. Ganesha said, with some reluctance, that they were prepared to help a town of predominately Anglo-Saxon heathens, on the basis that a shrine be erected in their honour. Fairness Man said that wouldn't be an issue, as the small rockery skirting the north of the Barry Towers garden pond would provide an excellent location for a suitable place to worship his excellence.

Fairness Man took his appetisers and informed Abdul that he would report back once he'd locked horns with the bureaucratic might of the council. While environmental regulations were one removed from my core expertise in housing policy administration and advanced filing systems, I'm sure there would be some transferable skills that could come to fruition. I would need to find time to do some web research to provide Fairness Man the necessary intellectual artillery he would need to fend off the officious, rules-obsessed, frustrated under-achievers who stalked the corridors of the Environmental Planning Department. People embittered by years of team meetings and draconian HR policy. Fairness Man will come, and you will be touched by his hand of compassion.

Fairness Man listened to the dependable chime of the Barry

Towers doorbell. There had being several doorbell sounds to choose from, ranging from 'Beethoven's 4th Symphony' to 'I'm Horny' by underrated Dutch pop-techno maestro Moose T, but I'd opted for the timeless and internationally recognised ding-dong. Nancy opened the front door and let out a deep sigh on seeing our caped righter of wrongs, followed by an outburst which included, comrades, brace yourself, what I would classify as a semi-swear.

'George, what the bloody hell are you up to? Have you lost complete control of your senses? And what's with the religious clothing? Have you mugged Reverend Ormerod or something?'

Fairness Man wasn't sure if Nancy, or the rest of the congregation gathered in the front room, were ready for the news. Nancy had always been noncommittal regards her religious beliefs, but I had my suspicions that she may be a closet believer. As for Sophie and Nathan, I doubted that a religious belief system had broken through the filter of their young, impressionable lives, but perhaps they had fallen under the spell of a phony guru, tempting them into their cult through a trendy brand of oat-milk smoothies. Rose would be a harder nut to crack, due to her dislike of Fairness Man and the cold, hard logic of life lived in the godless reality of Weyford. Even through the alcoholic haze, she could sniff out the bullshit of a false idol. She needed spirituality combined with substance. By melding the best of religion with the most advanced scientific thinking, grounded in an ideology for equality and change, he would pierce through her outer crust and shine a light into her soul.

The onion bhajis had whetted Fairness Man's hunger and, trying to divert the conversation away from the vicious tempest of animosity towards the pond of tranquillity, he asked if there was any dinner left.

'Yes, but I don't know why I haven't thrown it straight into the bin. Now get that fancy dress off and start acting your age.'

I could see that Nancy, after years of being spoilt by my dependable and progressive-minded presence, was struggling to keep up with Fairness Man's expansive worldview. Being ever-sensitive to Nancy's needs, he disappeared to the bedroom and disrobed. I, the right honourable George Barry, walked back out towards the living room, ready to play the messenger, to be the mouthpiece of a new god. Like Moses, I would hear his words and translate them into the language of the common man, woman or person.

I settled back in the living room, tray on lap and the comforting smell of bangers, mash and onion gravy helping my feet get back on the ground. I relayed Fairness Man's damascene journey and his unexpected reinvention as a left-leaning godhead. It was a lot to take on board, but when I bullet-pointed the Five Commandments in quick succession, there were one or two nods of support. Commandment Four, 'Never inflict harm on animals', resonated with the younger demographic, while the first three commandments, lifted straight from the original text, played to Nancy's more traditional values. Rose, with a Dubonnet-infused glint in her eye, criticised Commandment Five, 'We should all pay our fair share in creating a caring, cooperative society', as liberal bullshit, but I looked beyond the acerbic wit and saw that deep down she was broadly aligned to the overall direction of travel.

Nancy did question why a 'lifelong card-carrying atheist would develop a half-baked, narcissistic God complex'.

While her point was well made, I had to explain that, 'God, i.e. Fairness Man, moved in mysterious ways, and who are we to question a higher force?'

I decided to edit out the episode with Reverend Ormerod. While he was the victim of his own physical ineptitude, I had technically taken his garment without agreement. The pedants out there may consider this breaking the Second Commandment, but, comrades, that is the wonder of divine intervention. As Rasputin was a gift to Lenin, distracting and destabilising the already-unpopular Russian royal family, a hidden lower pole of a free-standing clothes rail had rewarded me with the key to the sartorial wardrobe of St Mary's Church.

The agenda shifted to popular entertainment and a group decision was made to watch *Mamma Mia* to 'lighten the mood' and take 'our minds off things'. I accepted the need for escapism and begrudgingly allowed myself a couple of hours' break to enjoy the ABBA-themed musical rom-com. Even hardened political animals like myself can enjoy 'Voulez-Vous' performed by ageing thesps on a beautiful Greek island, after a hard day's graft.

Rose turned out to be a musical fanatic. Her interests and life experiences never cease to amaze. 'Take a Chance on Me' was her favourite song in the film and she treated us all to an impromptu duet with Julie Walters, who she rightfully described as a 'fucking national treasure'. Bobby joined in on the chorus with a crescendo of barks. What a talent he is. If only we could bottle and reproduce his DNA, the world would be a better place.

After the joyous filmic diversion, we dispersed to our beds. As we tucked in for a good night's sleep, conversation between Nancy and me was absent. Fairness Man had driven something of a wedge between us, but I was sure that on a clear head and with the peace of the weekend to come, we would settle back into our normal state of amicable collaboration and bonhomie.

SATURDAY APRIL 3RD

I got up in a determined mood. I wasn't going to let the usual casual Saturday vibe slow the momentum that was building. As dear Lenny would say, a day's rest is a week lost. The mood over breakfast was upbeat, and I took this as an opportunity to delegate a range of suitable tasks to the different members of what I'm now billing Team Barry. We could be described as a modern family, but I prefer the word team, with its reassuring competitive undertones. We wouldn't just get on and cohabit; we would work to shared goals and achieve excellence by continually pushing in the same direction. They are the able oarsmen, women or people, and I'm the cox, upfront shouting, directing and urging them on to victory.

I checked in with Nathan and Sophie on the social-media front. They said my film 'hadn't taken off', with a modest 345 views. Perhaps I strayed beyond the mass market into the avant-garde with my poetic dance fusion. Not put off by this small setback, we broke into a quickfire brainstorm of content ideas. We needed to sell the new religious direction without alienating Fairness Man's established following. Our collective minds honed in on the Five Commandments. They were short, familiar and, as Sophie pointed out, 'relatable'. As we needed to shunt up our existing five commandments to a more respectable ten, Nathan suggested we 'crowdsource' the vacant spots in a sort of free-for-all internet prize draw. The lucky people whose commandments were selected would be made disciples and get a chance to meet the legend himself, Fairness Man. I was happy to give this idea the greenlight. I turned my attention to Nancy. As a rule, she wasn't one who liked to be delegated to. Erring on the side of caution, I suggested that she wash Fairness Man's newly acquired robe of worship. I needed to get rid of the faint stench of Ormerod, a nagging reminder of the old order.

She agreed on the basis that I wouldn't wear it again and 'make myself look like an imbecile'. I would never demean Fairness Man by seeking to imitate his unique fashion style, so was happy to accept the deal. I briefed Rose on the day's rehabilitation programme, which involved an hour of meditation following breakfast and a symposium on social theory in the afternoon. This would give her plenty of time to enjoy her comfortable surroundings. She said it sounded 'bloody dull, George', and that her and Nancy had decided they would spend some time together baking. While unconventional, I was prepared to accept cake making as a valuable component of my ideological ecosystem.

While it's great to be able to use my magnetic personality to engage and motivate those within Team Barry, it can at times feel like a curse. The emotional weight of dealing with their constant needs and demands is draining, and something akin to looking after a group of toddlers. Like a nursery manager, stinking of children's excrement and vomit, I needed to come up for air and find a neutral space for peaceful contemplation. Bobby was also at a loose end, and after a quick conversation, we agreed that a walk in the woods would meet our mutual needs. We both felt revived as we stepped outside and breathed in the cool morning air. Once in the woods, Bobby kept spotting and chasing after squirrels, their furry tails disappearing into bushes or scampering up the nearest tree. With not a soul in sight, I shared my feelings with my faithful friend. Under normal circumstances my first port of call would be Nancy, but we had reached an icy impasse in our otherwise well-functioning relationship, which needed a day or two to thaw in the warm glow of our love. Fairness Man was undoubtedly a barrier to a return to harmony. His presence had created what I can only describe as a love-hate triangle. I needed to double down on exuding and absorbing love vis-à-vis Nancy, to build a stockpile of good feeling that would drown out the hatred and resentment for him. Trying to explain this complex, emotionally charged conundrum to Bobby was a challenge, as his mind was fixed on his unsuccessful squirrel-hunting. I knew that he was taking in the gist of my consternation, but it would be nice to have a least a bit of eye contact or a bark or two aimed in my direction.

We carried on walking deeper into the woods, Bobby on his merry squirrel-obsessed dance and me honing my ears on the wide variety of birdsong, when I heard barking followed by the unmistakable tone of an irate middle-class male exclaiming, 'Get away from me you mutt!', followed by an Eastern European-sounding female, 'Shoo, shoo, you furry little pest.'

I ran over, agitating my bothersome hip, and got a sight I was not prepared for. There was the scrawny milk white arse of Mr Cheese glinting in the spring sun, who was caught, quite literally, with his trousers down and atop a woman who, I made an intelligent guess, from her accent and from my knowledge of the village gossip, was Tatiana, his Polish cleaner and mistress. She had a blonde perm and striking blue eyes set off by an interesting choice of purple eyeshadow. She tried to bat off Bobby as he licked her face, but he had taken a liking to her Eastern European charms. Tatiana was unperturbed by being caught in an al fresco sexual act on public land. There are probably different byelaws for this sort of thing in Poland, where a small bribe would normally sort out most disputes. She pushed the spindly limbed Mr Cheese aside, sending him rolling on to his back, giving me sight of his gentleman friend, thankfully no longer erect due to the unwanted canine disturbance.

His head nestled amongst a pile of leaves, eyes red with anger, he unfairly labelled me a, 'Dirty git, sneaking up on people in the woods. You should be ashamed of yourself, George.'

I tried to reassure him that having both the image of his front and rear private parts seared into my brain was the last thing I needed and that I would have to practise a daily ritual of image displacement techniques to edge his unsightly cock, balls and arse out of my visual memory banks. My optical trauma didn't stretch to Tatiana, who was way out of Mr Cheese's league and whose relationship with him was built on the cynical patriarchal exploitation of a monetary power dynamic. Tatiana pulled up her knickers, adjusted her leather mini-skirt and buttoned up her pastel-pink blouse. Even to my stylistically naive eye, I could see that her fashion sense was lost somewhere between 1982 and 1987. This was, as you well know, comrades, during my foray into the hedonistic bowels of Basildon. In this period, I kept an arm's length from the flamboyance of the New Romantics and their futile experimentation with gender identity and opted for the Farah slack and the Ben Sherman shirt. Solid British brands that matched my understated patriotism without straying into the choppy waters of nationalism. In these formative years, as I moved from a proto-adult to the well-rounded exemplar of progressive dynamism I am today, I had plenty of experience being ignored by women dressed like Tatiana but, as an easy-going pacifist, had avoided violent altercations. So when she slapped me hard on my right cheek, at such a force that I rocked back on my heels and just about managed to regain balance and avoid tumbling backwards into a thicket, I was stunned.

She cast further aspersions on my character, saying that, 'You are a sad little man, who should go back home to your sad little life of dressing up and stealing other people's drinks. In Poland we lock up people like you.'

I was taken aback by the brazen, unrepentant couple, and felt it was only my duty to get them up to speed on the new religious movement that now judged and guided their conduct. I explained that they would be pleased that the nascent moral code was open to different sexual orientations and identities, and non-discriminatory in its nature, but unfortunately for them adultery was a big no-no, as stipulated by Commandment Three. I could, however, offer them a get-out-of-jail-free card if they fancied. In hindsight, I should have been more direct in my choice of words, as I'm not sure that Monopoly had embedded itself in Polish popular culture. Tatiana was not willing to listen to my proposed deal of repentance that they sign up as disciples and co-workers, to add the necessary support needed to bolster the solitary and lacklustre figure of Rolly Peterson.

She said, 'Go and fuck yourself, you creep,' stomping off in the direction of Burhampton with the hunched figure of Mr Cheese following behind, declaring his undying love while pulling some stray leaves out of his hair.

It was plain to see that some people are beyond salvation. Mr Cheese and the multitudes like him would have to be tolerated but couldn't be expected to play an active role in a new society. With Mr Cheese's buttocks flickering in my mind's eye, inhibiting my normal intellectual efficiency, Bobby and I decided to cut our walk short and return to Barry Towers.

Nancy and Rose were busy baking fairy cakes and Nathan and Sophie were in the garden, practising what I'm guessing was yoga. With Team Barry occupied, I felt the urge to check the pulse of the local heartbeat of cyber chat. With great trepidation, I clicked open the Burhampton Forum, and what I found can only be described as a digital shitstorm: an omen for the challenges I was about to face. The axis of evil – the Spatchcocks, what we are now referring

130

to as the religion formerly known as the Church of England and the anonymous sniping trolls of life sapping negativity – had joined forces under a new discussion thread titled '*Ban Barry*'. Jesus, I know how it felt to have all sides turn on you, scared of your magnificence.

RevRightOn instigated the debate by writing that, '*I was robbed blind of my finest cassock. He has stolen church property, which is tantamount to mugging God. The man is out of control. I think we should take matters into our own hands and ban George Barry from every shop, pub and public space within the Burhampton Parish. He is a threat to our health and wellbeing and must be stamped out*.' This was met with universal approval.

TonyBeermeister took pride in stating that, '*I have already taken action. I have banned him from the pub, but the bastard has already sneaked back in. So keep your eyes peeled and we can stamp him out*.'

Wilko followed up to add that, '*His feral companion* [Rose], *should also be included in the ban, as she has an aggressive manner incongruous with Making Great Britain Great once more*.'

Their comments couldn't go answered anymore. It was time to place my head above the parapet and enter the fray. I created a profile with the username George Barry, not needing to hide behind the safety blanket of an online alter ego. I entered the '*Ban Barry*' discussion and clicked on the comment button. As I stared at the empty white box, I was overwhelmed with the responsibility of shouldering the burdens of a nation and sought guidance from Ganesha. Their centuries-old wisdom and all-round chilled outlook on everything, from famine to plagues, helped put things in perspective. They explained that no obstacle was insurmountable and that by harnessing my positive energy anything was achievable.

I'm a massive fan of positive energy, and except for my occasional bouts of melancholy, it is a quality I have in spades. If they wanted to exclude me, then so be it, I would build an alternative society in my image, free of their petty concerns and quibbles. There were some logistical challenges to overcome, such as where to pop to get a pint of milk, but Nancy would have to take over my responsibilities for top-up shopping. I would be free of any interactions with my foes and be able to operate uninterrupted in my own ecosystem. Feeling liberated, I penned the following statement:

> *It is me, George Barry, dedicated public servant, family man, campaigner, activist, author, political and religious leader. I have not been honoured with a title to date, but for the record, while I'm deserving of an OBE and, perhaps in time, a knighthood, I wouldn't except them for myriad reasons: including my opposition to the monarchy, elitism, vainglorious bourgeois constructs, nepotism, cronyism, class and gender bias. I have worked tirelessly these last few days to build something new. To redistribute the dirty spoils of capitalism; to provide an alternative path for the homeless; to protect our small businesses, the pillars of our communities; to dismantle and rebuild our outmoded and atrophied church. I've been ably assisted by Fairness Man in my work. A man who operates in ways that are beyond your understanding. While he has ruffled a few feathers through his unconventional manner, his aims have justified his means.*

We wanted, no matter how hard it may be, to find common ground, but you seek to ostracise us from Burhampton life. So be it: we shall build a better society from the ground up. For your interest I have Ganesha, the elephant-headed Indian god, providing spiritual guidance, and I'm lucky enough to have recruited Rolly Peterson as a disciple who will act as a vital link between your world and mine. Nancy will most likely want to lead as normal a life as possible, so I ask you to leave her be as she visits the shops, plays tennis or tends to her various social and charitable commitments. She is a supportive but semi-engaged member of Team Barry, so please let her roam freely. As for Rose, while she has anger-management issues, she will now be safely enclosed within Barry Towers, completing a programme of rehabilitation. My daughter Sophie and her partner, Nathan, will soon be returning to London, so not of your concern. That leaves dear Bobby, my forever smiling fluffy companion. You can berate, harass and harangue me, but he will provide the constant friendship that will raise my spirits in my darkest moments.

Kind regards,
George Barry

I closed the forum and wouldn't be returning. I went to the kitchen to tell Nancy of the inconvenience of being banned from Burhampton. She and Rose were in good spirits, chatting and listening to the radio as their cakes baked, so I decided it was best not to break the news. A sense of domestic harmony hung in the air and I felt blessed to have a warm shield of love in which to nurture something brighter, better and fairer. We'd have to be more self-sufficient, which was in tune with my ecological beliefs. Yes, we'd be a blueprint for a new way of living, delicately balancing socialism, progressive religion and domestic vegetable production. I'd need to dig up the lawn to create a vegetable patch, but it was a necessity now our access to multinational food industry supply chains was severed. Longer term we could invest in livestock – perhaps a few chickens and a couple of pigs – and ramp up our production capability. I would miss dropping by Tesco Express for a cheeky bag of doughnuts, but I'd be lining their pockets no more. In the meantime, where Nancy decided to shop, of course, was her own business.

My positive-energy reserves dwindled as the doorbell rang and I opened the door to two members of the police. They could have been mistaken for twin brothers, with their lumbering bodies, moon-shaped heads and squashed rugby-player noses.

They wanted to question me, 'About an incident involving yourself and Reverend Ormerod, may we come in?'

God damn it, that wretched excuse of a man had dobbed me in. So much for forgiveness, you little shit. I led them into the living room, where they could enjoy the comfort of the floral sofa. Nancy, startled by the presence of the two bobbies but ever-resilient, offered them both a nice cuppa and a freshly baked fairy cake. She knew it was important to soften up the old bill with the provision of treats. The twin coppers requested that she leave us in privacy. I could see Rose, naturally suspicious of the law, retreat to the shed for safety. Sophie and Nathan were engrossed in some form of aerobic activity in the garden and oblivious to proceedings.

The police didn't mince their words. 'So, Mr Barry, is it correct that you stole a piece of church property earlier today after a violent tussle with a member of the clergy, Reverend Timothy Ormerod?'

I explained to the police officers that the Reverend was 'prone to exaggeration and propagation of myth. It is an unfortunate by-product of being a man of the cloth and can't be helped'.

I said that, 'The person you need to speak to is Fairness Man, but as he is otherwise indisposed, I am happy to act as his legal advisor.'

I clarified that, 'The violent tussle was something akin to mano a mano Greco-Roman wrestling. An honourable art form where no punches and kicks were inflicted on the opposition. And the ultimate blow that led the Reverend to lose consciousness was a self-inflicted accident that is common amongst those who are physically challenged.'

I did admit that Fairness Man had acquired a cassock, but there were many to spare, and as a newly appointed god, he needed to be dressed accordingly.

This didn't pass muster, and the police informed me that, 'George Barry, we need to take you to Larton Police Station for further questioning.'

I explained that this was a case of mistaken identity and would go and get the miscreant they were looking for.

While I'm used to playing by the book, Fairness Man is not. I could advise him in matters of the law, but my influence only stretches so far. I went upstairs and, not wishing to delay the police in their work, put on mask, cape, neckerchief and cassock. As I predicted, Fairness Man took a different view on events. He didn't like false allegations being thrown in his direction and realised any further discussion with the coppers was futile. He'd have to live the life of a fugitive. In the ideal world, he'd opt for the Raleigh as his mode of transport, but that meant passing the policemen to access the garage, so he had to use an alternative exit point. He opened the bedroom window and eyed up the driveway. It was an easy descent for someone of his calibre. A man who, if given the opportunity, could develop a taste for parkour and assisted sky diving. He heard steps approaching the bedroom.

'Are you OK in there, Mr Barry? Please, we must go to the police station, we don't want to have to use force.'

The door opened, and Nancy walked in. 'Come to your senses, George, and get going, for crying out loud.'

Fairness Man took this as his cue and, grabbing the window ledge, flung his legs outside and hung above the ground, before making the drop of several feet to the tarmacked drive. He bent his knees to take the shock, but he felt a sharp pain in his dodgy hip and quickly had to come to terms with the difficult task that he had set himself. If, like a Russian Olympian, he had a ready supply of performance-enhancing drugs, he may have been able to overcome his impediment, but rifling through his pocket all he had was an old packet of Lockets and a crumpled receipt. The Lockets would help open his airways and offer a marginal improvement in his lung capacity, so were worth a try. He placed two Lockets in this mouth, and while the menthol vapours provided a pleasant sensation in both throat and nostrils, as he attempted to run down the driveway, it soon became apparent that they offered no help in alleviating hip pain. Realising that he would not be able to outrun the police, he looked for somewhere to hide. The only place nearby that could accommodate him was a green wheelie recycling bin. He tilted the bin towards himself to give easy access to entry. He placed one leg inside and pushed up with the other leg to tilt the bin back to an upright position. He swung his other leg over and crouched down on top of the food packaging and tin cans. He tried to shut the lid, but there was not enough room for it to close, leaving a gap of one to two inches from which he could be spotted. If only I had been less diligent in my recycling habits, Fairness Man would have been undetectable. I'm sorry, old chum, the planet comes first.

The front door opened, and the two policemen and Nancy walked out. Fairness Man closed his eyes and imagined a technological utopia where he'd mastered the power of invisibility and the police had been replaced by robots with a superior grasp of the nuances involved in effective law enforcement, rather than witless fools chasing crime statistics so their chief can get a pay rise and afford to pay for the extension he's always dreamed of. In this utopia, our squash-nosed cops would be free to have more leisure time and survive on a universal basic income. This brilliantly conceived, high-functioning imagined world was destroyed as one of the lumpen twins swung open the bin, pulled out one of Fairness Man's arms and fixed a handcuff to his wrist. The policeman fixed the other cuff to one of his own wrists, moved the bin to the floor and pulled Fairness Man out. He realised that any form of resistance was futile and, in a rare bout of silence, was taken into the back seat of the police car.

Nancy shed a tear of sadness and relief. 'It'll be OK, don't worry, darling. Just do as the kind men say.'

It was admirable that Nancy respected the pillars of the establishment, but she could at least be on Fairness Man's side and proclaim his innocence. She just couldn't get past his brash exterior and appreciate his inner qualities.

As the police car pulled away from Barry Towers, it passed the ogling grimace of Chinny Wilkinson, who, like a tabloid photographer sniffing out a scandal, lifted up his phone and took a picture of the detained superhero. I wouldn't expect anything less from a man who'd ran the British public transport system into the ground under the guise of competition, through a fractured franchise model that banished the buffet carriage: a vital service that supported a generation of functioning commuting alcoholics and replaced it with a sea of misery.

As they made the journey to Larton Police Station, Fairness Man broke the silence by humming 'In the Air Tonight' by Phil Collins. He felt its poignant soft-rock feel encapsulated the longing, loss and anguish he was experiencing and hoped he could invoke a degree of empathy from the police twins that would go in his favour. While their emotional intelligence was at the bottom of the spectrum, he was banking on eighties pop being a suitable medium which they could relate to. As he reached the peak of the protracted intro and broke into the epic drum roll, the twin he was handcuffed to asked him to be quiet, as musical performance was prohibited within registered police vehicles. Not to be outdone, he carried on by mentally humming the remaining three verses and choruses that made up this adult-orientated rock classic.

Fairness Man was marched past the reception desk and taken to a room for questioning. It was the type of room he was familiar with from TV crime dramas but had never experienced first-hand. The twins left the room and a few minutes later entered a man who introduced himself as Police Sergeant Button. He had no visible body hair and his steel-blue eyes stood out from his milk-white blob of a head. He had the air of a man in desperate need of a break but who, through a deluded sense of self-worth, thought it would all go to pot if he left Larton Police Station unattended.

'So, Mr Barry, you are our very own superstar petty thief. Captain Cappuccino, or should it now be Captain Cassock? Think you're clever, do you?'

Fairness Man clarified that he didn't think he was clever; he knew that he was clever, on the basis that his IQ would easily qualify for Mensa, even though he'd been too busy to date to complete the necessary test. He was not in the mood for the tedium of cross-examination and admitted to stealing the cassock. Sergeant Button thanked him for his honesty and questioned him further on whether he used physical force to obtain the garment. He explained, once again, what had happened and pointed Sergeant Button in the direction of the Burhampton Forum if he wanted any evidence of a man who didn't have a firm grip on reality.

'So, are you calling Reverend Ormerod, a trusted member of the clergy, a liar, Mr Barry?'

'Less of a liar, more of a fantasist. A man who has spent too much time living in his own bubble, fermenting imagined plots and conspiracies.'

'So, would you describe an ageing man wearing a black cape and mask, and a red neckerchief, as someone with a firm grasp of reality?'

Fairness Man was well prepared for a forensic character examination and was aware that his unconventional appearance was outside Sergeant Button's usual frame of reference. In Sergeant Button's world you either wore normal clothes or you were a weirdo with a high propensity to be a deviant recidivist. We can hope that the robot police force of the future will have in-depth understanding of modern identity politics and not be blighted by these narrow-minded prejudices. I look forward to the day that these shiny metallic bobbies are gliding down the thoroughfares of Burhampton, wishing passing citizens good day, providing the reassurance that law and order was safe in their programmed hands.

Fairness Man made it clear that his disguise was an important means of anonymity that enabled him to protect the rights of those in need, without falling into the egotistical and narcissistic trappings of fame. He explained that he had recently taken on the mantle from the Church of England as the nation's default religion and that the cassock was merely a semiotic embellishment to signal this to people, without the need for sermons or a reworked Alpha course.

Sergeant Button said that he didn't, 'Have a clue what you are on about. But on the basis that I have no evidence the attack took place, that the theft is a petty crime and you have never offended before, I'm going to caution you on this occasion. Mr Barry, please remove the cassock and then you are free to leave. Don't fuck about again, as the consequences will be far graver.'

Fairness Man thanked Sergeant Button for his excellent judgment and offered him a chance to expand his extra-curricular activity and become a disciple. I don't think he is a religious man, as he responded, 'Please leave now, I have work to do.'

Fairness Man stepped out of the interrogation room, breathed the sweet air of freedom and flexed the muscles of emancipation. He was granted one phone call, so he rang Barry Towers to relay the good news and request a lift home.

Nancy was relieved and asked Fairness Man, 'Can we all put this behind us now and move on with our lives?'

He agreed and looked forward to the next harmonious chapter of life.

Nancy picked him up in the Astra. He sat in the passenger seat and removed his disguise. The tension subsided as we drove off and I put on the radio. I quickly retuned it from Radio 4 to Surrey Easy Vibes, a lesser-known DAB offshoot of Surrey Golden Oldies, and it didn't let me down. 'Something Inside So Strong' by Labi Siffre was playing – an all-time classic by anyone's reckoning. We shared a smile and it felt like the good times were around the corner.

With the unnecessary police incursion fading into the past, Nancy took the opportunity to remind me that I needed to find a home for Rose.

I said that, 'I think a deep bond is forming between you both and it would be a shame to break it apart at a fledging stage, which would put Rose's rehabilitation into jeopardy and throw her back into a world of uncertainty, addiction and domestic abuse.'

Nancy said, 'I like Rose, but she needs proper support, which we can't provide.' I tried to explain that support for

141

the homeless was central to the services I was now offering, but she poured cold water on the vision ablaze within me. 'George, you don't know what you're doing. Please find someone who does.'

I bought some time by saying I would be on it first thing Monday morning, after a well-needed rest on Sunday, the holy day.

Sophie gave me a big hug on my return to Barry Towers. 'Are you OK? It must have been horrible.'

I said that Fairness Man was thick-skinned and more than a match for the middle-management of Larton Police, who soon came to the realisation that a cautionary slap on the wrist was sufficient punishment. While the official law-making channels had been nullified, it was a different situation online, where the cesspit of digital media was its own judge and jury. Chinny had fired the picture of Fairness Man, sitting forlorn in the police car, in several directions, and in the short time he had been incarcerated, it had made its way onto the website homepage of the *South West Surrey Observer* with the headline 'Captured Cappuccino Loses His Froth'. The article was outdated and factually incorrect, linking the arrest to his coffee-redistribution programme while making no reference to cassocks. No wonder mainstream media was going down the tubes with this sort of piss-poor reporting. I strayed into the comments section, but it was like opening the door into a cavern of lunatics, locked in their rooms, starved of light, company and reason, and inflicting their negative bile on the world.

Barrybob24 described me as, '*a senile loony, who deserves to be kicked out of the country along with all the other spongers*'.

RaraRodney said, '*It is time to bring back the death*

penalty to sort out this sort of behaviour, once and for all'.

Sophie and Nathan said that Fairness Man's arrest hadn't had an impact on his popularity amongst the faithful, slightly dwindling, younger, metropolitan fanbase, with several comments calling for him to be freed. The crowdsourcing of the Five Commandments was also going relatively well, with two entries received so far. We had a quickfire brainstorm and added a few more options to help us bump things up to the magnificent ten neo-biblical rules that we required. We reviewed the potential commandments and placed them into three groups: No Way, Possibly and Definitely.

No Way

Thou shall have kale smoothies only on Tuesdays (Sophie and Nathan's suggestion. Not a beverage of my choice, but I believe in a liberal approach to healthy drink consumption).

Thou shall not be allowed to wear socks with sandals (sorry, Janita from Hull, but you are overruled, as what you state as a *'fashion crime'* is in fact a practical and underrated combination providing an aerated yet warm foot that is well suited to the temperate climate of the UK and can be utilised for between seven and nine months of the year).

Possibly

Thou shall not end a sentence with the word right, as it creates a leading statement putting pressure on the recipient to agree. It is an irritating, passive-aggressive cry for self-affirmation that needs to be banished (OK, this one came from me. It faced some resistance from Sophie and Nathan, who, as prime offenders of using this infuriating verbal tick, didn't see the problem).

Thou shall practise thirty minutes of meditation a day (OK, me again. Sophie and Nathan pushed back again saying meditation was dull, and that yoga or Pilates are more beneficial as you are exercising your body, while relaxing the mind. The benefits of stillness were lost on them).

Definitely
Thou shall be respectful of other people's needs (clear, memorable and brilliant. Thanks, Lucy from Portsmouth, Fairness Man will be in touch about meeting up. How will it feel to be a disciple? Pretty awesome, I imagine).

Thou shall listen to your inner voice and not slavishly follow the stereotypical expectations placed on you from your formative years onward (this was a collaboration. I built on the inner voice element by, fittingly, listening to my inner voice, to complete the commandment).

The commandments were shaping up nicely, and we all agreed that as Saturday evening drew nearer that it was time to chill. I am not a natural chiller, but the strain of acting as legal advisor to Fairness Man had taken its toll, plus my aching hip needed some relief from the continued physical pressure that had been put upon it. Nancy ordered a takeaway curry, providing an essential cash injection for The Golden Tandoori and a much-deserved treat for Team Barry. She said she was pleased that 'the old George is back'. I wasn't quite sure what she was getting at but nodded in agreement.

Rose, ever to the point, asked, 'Are you going to stop wearing that stupid costume and acting like a dick?'

Not wanting to end the day on a low point, I steered the conversation away from Fairness Man and towards the communal anaesthetic otherwise known as TV. That turned out to be a mistake, as the live final of *Sun, Sex, Hook Up or Get Lost* was on. Everyone, except me, soon became engrossed in the carnal web of the narcissistic pond life vying for their five minutes of fame. I tried to engage with the perma-tanned discussions of who fancied who, when I had a sensation that I was floating in space, being slowly dragged into an alternative dimension without meaning or physical form. I drifted in this state until the arrival of my chicken jalfrezi. Its perfect blend of spices pulled me back into the sentient world, where everyone was still glued to the TV. I don't think Lenny would have tolerated the titillating frivolity of the libidinous reality format. My approach is more open and inclusive, bridging the gap between highbrow intellectual nourishment and lumpen proletarian light entertainment.

The curry was followed by a chocolate fudge cake baked by Nancy and Rose. The unctuous goo was the perfect counterpoint to the fiery delights that had preceded it. I had provided the ideal environment for Rose to wade out of the quagmire of dirt she had been bathing in for years. She had emerged like the lady in the lake, a baking tour de force, whose sugar-infused skills had no limits. That she had reached such heights, despite frequent lapses into inebriation, was testament to her talent. Nancy was understanding of the snaky path to sobriety, having weaned me off my real ale habit in the early days of our courtship. On my wilder occasions, I may have reached the dizzy heights of an eight-pint haul. But after one too many disappearances down the dark reaches of vomit avenue, Nancy's high-grade support skills had reigned things back to a four-pint limit, with an allowance for a gin and tonic on special occasions. Nancy had insisted that Rose not drink before five o'clock and had bought her low-strength cider to temper her evening intake. It was paying off, as not only was the cake exceptional but Rose's temper was under control and her swear level had dropped down a notch or two. She did lack a filter when it came to matters of a sexual nature, which lead to the sort of comment not hitherto heard in the communal areas of Barry Towers. When Nancy asked Rose what she meant by nuts-deep, I knew it was time to say goodnight to Team Barry, charge down the George Barry power source and enter into a seven- to eight-hour period of unconscious recuperation.

SUNDAY APRIL 4ᵀᴴ

Yes, comrades, it is the holy day. Despite being an atheist, I was feeling spiritually uplifted. I upped the churchy vibes by putting a Sunday service on the radio and had breakfast as the rest of the team enjoyed a lie-in. It was the day of worship and Fairness Man had a responsibility to talk to the church-goers of Burhampton. They needed to be enlightened on the new change in direction regarding their religious beliefs. While it would be helpful to commandeer the church for the morning, it would most probably infringe on some outmoded law. Fairness Man needed a different arena in which to communicate. He was gaining more confidence in his performance skills and by offering an experimental approach to conveying his neo-theo-socio-political mantras, he could draw them away from the, let's face it, sanctimonious tone of the Bible. The people needed something that was bang up to date and a bit less preachy.

As I finished my cornflakes, my ears tuned into the sermon on the radio and found the words he needed: 'Go and eat delicacies and drink sweet drinks and send portions to those for whom nothing is prepared. For this day is holy to our Lord.' Yes, comrades, I had a moment of revelation: there in front of me were a box of delicacies in the form of fairy cakes. Reverend Ormerod was too busy tapping away his vile comments to selflessly prepare anything for his congregation. We could send his people portions of the cakes baked with love by a homeless artisan in collaboration with a matriarchal titan.

I sneaked into the bedroom and metamorphosed into Fairness Man without waking Nancy. He wheeled the Raleigh out of the garage and placed the box of fairy cakes in the trailer. His hip let out a gentle sigh of relief as he sat on his source of two-wheeled mechanical joy. He ran the current list of seven commandments through his head a couple of times, ready to reel them off if the opportunity emerged. He pedalled at a steady pace, knowing that time was on his side, as due to the perfunctory information provided on www.godisgreat-stmarys.co.uk, he'd ascertained that the service wouldn't be starting for another half an hour. He got to the church and found a vantage point on the other side of the road, by a large tree. From here he could hide if Reverend Ormerod emerged and intercept people on their way to listen to another week of his half-witted dirge. He opened up the box of fairy cakes, ready to entice Ormerod's flock. He took a moment's rest, sitting behind the tree, and thought it only correct that he say his prayers. His most recent reference point was praying, unsuccessfully, for Southend to be victorious in the third round of the Johnstone's Paint Trophy. This left a sour prayer-related taste in his mouth, which he needed to rinse out with the sweet taste of a progressive and holistic belief system.

Dear George, Ganesha and Lenny. I pray that you will always support me in every act, no matter how small or insignificant (even though we are all well aware that 95% of my life is highly significant and influential in myriad ways that are hard to quantify but, nevertheless, if someone had the time and inclination to calculate, it would quite literally be off the carefully chosen and scientifically calibrated scale). I pray for the good people of Burhampton to open their ears and mouths and sample the theo-psychological and gastronomic delights I will share with them today. I pray that Reverend Ormerod stops being threatened by my presence and reins in his operations, paving the way for shared access to his consecrated habitat. I pray for the safety of Team Barry and my two disciples, Rolly and Lucy from Portsmouth. I pray that Lucy, despite the physical distance, will prove of greater assistance than the amiable but middling Mr Peterson. I pray for productive discourse with Surrey County Council's Chief Environmental Officer. I pray that they have a free window in which I can impart the vital information needed to maintain the curry supply chain in Burhampton. I pray in thanks for Nancy's undying love.

Fairness Man stopped, as he felt the prayer count was getting out of hand and may exceed realistic expectations. Looking at the fairy cakes, he regretted not having had a more substantial breakfast. He'd cut out the full English to keep a lid on his creeping cholesterol levels. While it had benefited his arteries, it did lead to unannounced energy dips. He gave

Jesus maximum kudos for not giving in to temptation, but he didn't have access to the range of sweet treats that had burgeoned in the era of mass-produced convenience foods. If Jesus had a packet of chocolate digestives nagging at him from the biscuit tin, he would have taken his eye off healing the sick to have the occasional snack. With that in mind, he justified tucking into a fairy cake, leaving a full eleven cakes for public consumption. That was more than enough, as he had decided not to offer them to the morbidly obese. For this important sub-group, the gospel would be updated to read, 'And Lord God did remove the offer of sweet treats on medical grounds which support longer life expectancy and reduce the burden on the already overstretched health system.' Fairness Man championed the welfare state but was conversant with the need for well-placed incentives and interventions to empower people to lead healthier lives. He hated to discriminate in this way but had no choice in a world where neo-liberal economics had stacked the scales with crisps, pasties and chips in favour of the multinational food conglomerates.

Brushing the crumbs of temptation from his mouth, he spied his first potential converts. They were a couple of familiar geriatrics with whom he'd never had the pleasure of being introduced. They wore his and hers grey slacks, grey cardigans, and white shirts. The woman had her hair cut to a length of three to four inches longer than her male counterpart, to avoid confusion at an afternoon tea dance or a police line-up. He made a rough calculation of their BMI based on height and girth, that they were on the cusp of being overweight but a couple of stone clear of obesity.

As they came near him, they turned to cross the road

towards St Mary's Church. A short, pedestrian shuffle they had performed every Sunday for the past thirty-four years, except when away on their yearly one-week holiday to Salcombe in late May to early July.

He took a cake in each hand and crossed the road to block their path towards the church. 'Hello, dear folk, I'm Fairness Man, and I offer you these delicacies, for I am the Lord and I want to share God's love with you.'

The couple introduced themselves as Dot and Jon but politely turned down his offer, as, 'We are on a diet at the moment, doctor's orders and all that.'

He praised them on their ability to place scientific advice over religious doctrine. He informed them that he had supplanted the Church of England and created a valid alternative for those who understand the inherent hypocrisy within the current construct, as epitomised by Reverend Ormerod. He didn't have an alternative place of worship as yet, but he was planning a live stream on Instagram soon.

Dot said, 'It all sounded very interesting. Good luck with it.'

Fairness Man stressed that, 'Can't you see that I am the Lord? Think of me as a more switched-on version of Jesus. Yes, I've got the meek covered, but I have a more rounded view of political systems and the environmental crisis. Someone capable of negotiating with the higher echelons of Roman society and evading crucifixion.'

Jon said, 'God bless, we must be on our way,' and headed down the path of damnation.

They had a living deity smack bang in their face, plus free cake, and they turned it down for the ideological slavery of Ormerod, drip-feeding them a code of obedience, subservience and conformity. It was obvious that they were brainwashed, having fallen prey to his exploitative hypnotic gaze.

Fairness Man needed to switch approach and aim for the floating voter of Burhampton: the religiously noncommittal and undecided. People who got married in a church, because it's nice, and contemplated the existence of a higher force when the mood took them. He crossed back over the road and counted a further forty-five attendants for the morning's service, with not a Spatchcock in sight. With a population of approx. 3,000, there were swathes of idle minds to infiltrate. Fairness Man placed the fairy cakes back in the box and headed for the residential backstreets.

He roused the people of Burhampton from their slumber with a clear, concise and resonant mantra blended with the Pavlovian chimes of an ice-cream van, by using circular breathing techniques learnt whilst taking part in a native Australian outback experience in a suburb of Perth. The experience was run by Ron, who'd emigrated from Glasgow in the 1990s. What he lacked in indigenous credibility, he made up for with a ready supply of cold lager, or coldies, as he liked to call them. The experience was livened up with recollections of Old Firm football hooliganism. Ron, a Rangers fan and former member of the Inter City Firm, was pretty handy in his day, but following an extended time backpacking in South Asia, and a shift from Tennent's lager to marijuana, had realigned his life goals.

'Come and eat the cakes of peace, bing, bong, bing, have a little chat with me, the new-born king, bing, bong, bing, the cakes were made with the hands of a former homeless person's graft, bing, bong, bing, someone who rarely has the chance for a bath, bing, bong, bing, I've got some new commandments I think you'll like, bing, bong, bing, I'll sing you an abridged version while I ride my bike, bing, bong, bing. No murder, no nick, no philander, show the animals no harm, pay your fair share, cooperate and be calm, have respect for others' needs, bring stereotypical expectation to its knees.'

Fairness Man's sultry tones caught the ears of a smartly dressed woman, replete in a black woollen coat, red silk scarf and brown leather boots, out walking her dog, contemplating her existence and what was for lunch. He could see from the look in her eye that she had been lured into his belief system through his improvised riff and intermittent bing, bongs. She accepted one of the fairy cakes and thanked him for his kindness.

He asked if she was prepared to make some radical changes to her life to support the grassroots regeneration of the local area, incorporating a reimagining of places of worship.

She didn't want to be forced into a decision, but I could see she had started the gestation period to be reborn as a true believer.

She said that, 'The cake is delicious. Did you make it yourself?'

He was annoyed that she hadn't listened to the lyrics of his mantra, and so repeated the relevant lines in a slow dinner jazz style that would be easier to understand.

'The cakes were made with the hands of a former homeless person's graft, bing, bong, bing, someone who rarely has the chance for a bath, bing, bong, bing.'

This time, Fairness Man's acapella delivery flowed into her eardrums and had an immense impact. Connecting the poetic harmony with the sugary pleasure of the cake, she had a moment of epiphany.

'Well, it might be that someone's lucky day. My name's Sandra Smythe, and I own Burhampton Bakers, and I'm looking for new staff.'

I was surprised that I didn't recognise Sandra from my many a sausage-roll sojourn but put this down to the splendour of their glass displays, which filled my heart with delight and stopped me from paying due consideration to the bakery staff. Fairness Man gave Rose a glowing recommendation. He explained that she was a trained pastry chef, and as she now had access to the gamut of domestic amenities, her personal hygiene had reached acceptable levels.

'Well, tell her to come in for an interview tomorrow at nine in the morning. I look forward to meeting her. Nice to meet you, I best be off.'

He was impressed with Sandra's direct style. She was a captain of industry, who, once able to grasp the full remit of my social spiritual tsunami of wholesale recalibration, would make an excellent leader of business strategy (who also understood the importance of a nice buttered slice of toasted sourdough). We may be faced with environmental devastation, but you'll always be able to rely on a tasty bap to get you through the bleakest of days.

It was Fairness Man's first holy day, and he'd already pulled off one miracle. Jesus had to graft for years as a carpenter before he reached miracle status. In a supernatural head-to-head there was no contest.

He cycled back to Barry Towers to tell them the good news, but through the light came the darkness in the shape of Jeremy Simmonds, stepping out onto his gravel drive, his coal-black pupils showering disdain wherever their gaze settled. As he placed his golf clubs in the boot of the Aston Martin, he saw Fairness Man cycling by.

'I don't know what you're looking so happy about, Barry, we will slowly crush your spirits, freezing you out of all that is good about this Great British village for Great British people. People like you are dragging this country down, Barry, down into the pits of hell.'

Fairness Man had a good mind to correct him, but thought better and stuck to a, 'Toodle-oo, can't hear you, old bean,' as he whizzed by with his head held high.

He was soon back at Barry Towers and afforded himself a further fairy cake as a reward for his morning's efforts. He'd cast the net of the good word out into the choppy seas of Burhampton and returned with the catch of a whopping great job opportunity for Rose, in addition to having set the foundations for a grassroots movement. While he didn't have any new followers, in the truest sense, his words had percolated the air particles and would linger, ready to be inhaled by passing souls. They would breathe in the clean air of kind deeds, of generosity, sharing and support.

He knew his popularity ratings were at an all-time low within Barry Towers so made the selfless decision to sneak upstairs to our bedroom, undress and let myself take over. While his spiritual powers faded, I retained the feeling of success, which I aimed to inject into the psychological veins of Team Barry through the bearing of great news.

Nancy asked, 'Where have you been? We were worried that you might have had another one of your funny turns.'

I told her to fret not, as I had never felt better and, in fact, was approaching a state of elation.

'The delicious products of your domestic labour have been shared. Fairness Man took them out into the world. For he shone the light onto his love in all its wonder.'

Nancy said that, 'Nobody wants to see your love in all its wonder. Not even me, and I'm your wife.'

'That is where you are wrong, my dear. As Fairness Man's love spread out its tentacles and wrapped them around a superb opportunity in the form of an interview for Rose at Burhampton Bakers, tomorrow morning.'

The penny finally dropped, and Nancy had to admit to herself the genius of Fairness Man. He was unpredictable, and some might say a liability, but he delivered results.

Rose had taken Bobby for a walk in the woods, so I decided to track them down and tell them the good news. As I strolled through the undergrowth, I cursed Mr Cheese and Tatiana for tainting my associations of this fine public acreage. If only they had the decency of keeping their sordid affair behind closed doors, I could perambulate without the thought of their intertwined bodies. Using a mindfulness technique that I describe as nature-imbued synthesis, I purged these polluted thoughts and found inner harmony by focusing on the sway of the branch and rustle of the leaf, as the winds of change blew through this ancient land.

Mind cleansed, I walked on, when I saw Rose and Bobby coming towards me. In times gone by, Bobby would have run up to greet me, but as he remained by Rose's side,

I could see his loyalties were divided. If I'm to share his love, then so be it. You may have two masters, Bobby, but remember who was first, who cared and nurtured you from puppy to full-grown hound. I realise Rose is reaping the rewards of your companionship and the solace you bring. How could I deny that to another?

Me, man, and them, woman and dog, exchanged pleasantries, before I got down to business. I told Rose that, 'Fairness Man had used his religious launch pad to fire a rocket into the local job market, where it orbited a star, named Sandra Smythe, proprietor of Burhampton Bakers. She'd like to interview you for a job as a pastry chef. If successful, it could propel you into a galaxy of gainful employment and the associated benefits of purpose, self-worth and a monetary income.'

Rose was silent. I could see she feared success. That horrible feeling of dread and anxiety when faced with responsibility. Sister, I know what it's like to hit rock bottom. For years I shied away from the greasy pole of ambition in the dog-eat-dog world of Basildon Council Housing Department, but one day I woke up and realised my potential. I worked hard in creating the best filing system that department, and, to my best knowledge, all related departments, had ever witnessed and reached the position of Team Leader. If it wasn't for John Moffat taking credit for my work and cynically blocking my inexorable trajectory to the top of the housing department pyramid, through his insidious strain of passive-aggressive bullying, it would have been a different story. I looked into her eyes and searched for an answer.

'Thanks, George, I'll give it a fucking go.'

I commended Rose for her courage and pencilled in a coaching session on interview techniques for the afternoon.

'Interview techniques. Sounds like a load of bullshit.'

Yes, it was a necessary load of bullshit for the modern age.

The last interview I'd had was in 1998, so I would need to brush up on the finer detail of what was expected nowadays. Nancy had already, true to form, excelled in supporting Rose, helping her rekindle a love for baking. That was the essential element covered off, we now had to work on the extraneous and superficial elements that, unfortunately, count for a lot in this unforgiving world where talent alone is not enough, and people are developing their own 'personal brand'. Sophie and Nathan would be of great assistance, as they were immersed in modern work lingo and etiquette. Rose's insistence on using expletives to emphasise a point or merely to fill a gap, would need to be ironed out, but we had time.

On a normal Sunday, I would take the helm and steer the good ship roast dinner towards a harbour of crunchy potatoes, a succulent cove of chicken, before heading to the high seas of selected seasonal vegetables, smothered in the best gravy that money can buy (Bisto, obviously), but today I tossed the chef's hat to Nancy, where it nestled on her coiffured head.

I briefed Sophie and Nathan to compile a crib sheet of buzzwords and responses to the type of interview questions that Rose may be asked. Rose headed, without request, to the kitchen, where she would hone her skills preparing dessert. With the team occupied, I returned to my rightful position of master strategist. I set to work on scenario planning for the interview, when I was rudely interrupted by a text message from Rolly P, or the Rollster, as I was thinking of calling him. I eschewed the world of text whenever possible, on the basis that it lacked the nuance of the tongue, or the long-form pallet of the email or essay. I had long realised it was the default mode of communication in a world where people evaded verbal communication, finding an emotional connection through a well-placed emoji and the overuse of the exclamation mark.

It read, '*Sorry about the "Ban Barry" stuff. Be prepared, they are going to put posters up around town with your face on it. They've come up with a catchy slogan, "Don't interact with him. Don't serve him. Don't encourage him." I'm sure it will all blow over. Let me know if you need any essential supplies.*'

I'd touched the heart of this feeble man, and he was paying me back two-fold with this breaking intel. '*Agent Peterson. Excellent intelligence. Keep the pipeline of information flowing. May your star of principled subterfuge shine brightly.*'

After a superb lunch (roasties could have been a tad crispier, but nobody's perfect), Team Barry got down to some interview practice. After some initial hesitance, Rose said she would give it a try. Sophie and Nathan's crib sheet covered a broad spectrum of relevant and irrelevant questions; it was important that we were prepared for all eventualities.

'Where do you see yourself in five years' time?'

'Hopefully not dead,' said Rose.

While this deviated from Sophie and Nathan's advice to spell out your career goals in a punchy statement, I admired its brutal honesty and connection with the survival instinct that lurks within us all. I suggested that Rose mention, that through the pastoral care and the political-spiritual guidance provided at Barry Towers, her life expectancy is predicted to improve exponentially.

'What is your biggest life achievement?'

Rose was right to question, 'What the fuck does that have to do with making cakes?'

Sophie explained that potential employees just 'like to get to know you a bit'. She suggested that we try another one. 'OK, what would you say are your best qualities?'

Rose was not keen on answering these personality-based questions. Her tongue did loosen under the influence of alcohol, but as her rehabilitation coach, I could not recommend its use in any work situations. I suggested that she just be herself and say the first thing that comes into her head. With that in mind, we took it back from the top.

'What is your biggest life achievement?'

This time she was to the point: 'Making fucking great cakes.'

We all agreed this was a good response except for the thorny issue of the F bomb. It was time for me to make use of my mental toolkit to re-programme Rose's brain patterns and remove the full extent of her swearing glossary from her sentence construction.

I had started a night class of Beginner's Level Hypnotherapy at Basildon Technical College approximately ten years ago but had dropped out, as I felt the pace and depth of teaching didn't match my requirements. I did contemplate pole-vaulting into the intermediary-level course, but other things took over and the opportunity was lost. I jogged my memory by watching a quick online video tutorial from 'King Aziz, leading guru of matters of the mind, based in Wisconsin, USA. Family man, pancake lover, the views you see here are mine and don't represent those of my employer, Mid-West Chemcore'. I don't want to belittle the hypnotherapy brigade, but within a few minutes I was armed with all that was necessary for the basic reprogramming of the brain, which I would apply with haste to the eradication of bad language from dear Rose. The verbal effluent that had built up through twenty-three turbulent years would be unblocked and sloshed out, leaving purity of mind and tongue.

I grabbed a pen and pad, and beckoned Rose to the shed, where I would be free to manipulate her unconscious by sticking strictly to King Aziz's code of practice: never to hypnotise for your own entertainment, e.g. getting to bark like a dog, etc.; it's an unregulated field of study, so give it your best shot and don't forget to enjoy pancakes.

I explained to Rose that I was going to apply hypnosis to help her with the finer points of verbal communication.

She resisted, saying, 'Don't think I talk proper, do ya?'

I reassured her that wasn't the case, but said, 'You just need to use a few less swear words, Rose. While I'm fine with it, there are many who don't have the same liberal attitudes to the English language.'

I could tell from Rose's clenched teeth that she was holding in her feelings and wanted to tell me to fuck right off. The process of verbal reprogramming had begun.

I folded out a sun lounger, dusty from months of inactivity, and placed it in front of the shed. I asked Rose to lay down and I sat beside her on a humble striped deckchair.

A chair with sturdy frame and sturdy values. This was the sort of Britishness the Spatchcocks should champion: fine, functional, indiscriminate and sedentary. A chair for enjoying the sun but without a reclining function, thus enabling short naps but not the extravagance of the continental siesta.

I instructed Rose to shut her eyes. I needed to create a state of tranquillity, so she would be susceptible to 'going under'. There was a fresh wind blowing, so I fetched a blanket and placed it over her. King Aziz had recommended playing his own composition of ambient vibes, 'Dolphin Serenade at Midnight', but as we were in the garden without the necessary internet connectivity, this was not possible, so I opted for some sultry humming to the tune 'Islands in the Stream' by dear old Dolly Parton, ably accompanied by Kenny Rogers. I interjected the smooth melody of the pop country classic with hypnotic commands.

'You are now feeling sleepy, hmm, hmm, hmm, you are entering a safe place of mind manipulation, hmm, hmm, hmm, you are totally relaxed and ready to be put under my spell, hmm, hmmm, hmmm, hmm, hmm, hmm.'

I reached the last chorus and my hums faded to silence. As far as I could tell, Rose was ready to be hypnotised. Nancy had taken it upon herself to choose this exact moment to start weeding the flowerbeds. She had the portable radio and was enjoying the pleasant tones of Classic FM – a musical genre which provided a suitable backdrop for the hypnotism that was about to take place.

I started the hypnosis by giving Rose some background information on what was about to happen. 'I will start by probing into your use of swear words, why you use them and how they make you feel.'

Nancy looked over, and while she knew I was unqualified to undertake such procedures, any urge to halt my attempts to tinker with Rose's psyche was overridden by her pathological dislike of bad language.

'I will then use a system where we will replace any profanity with an innocuous replacement word, a word that will bring safety to your vocabulary and dissipate potential animosity that could arise in social situations. So, Rose, let us begin. Firstly, what is your favourite swear word and why?'

Rose, eyes closed, responded immediately, 'Piss, because it sounds like what it is,' her voice slow and mellifluous.

She was right; there was an onomatopoeic pleasure to be had in uttering this excellent and effective expletive. I wanted to commend her choice but resisted, as it would confuse the hypnotic process.

I asked how swearing made her feel and she said, 'It helps me get rid of my anger.' This was tricky. Her use of bad language was a vital anger-management tool. Without it her seething rage would overflow. I would weave a tried and tested visualisation technique into this hypno-programming session. This was leftfield of King Aziz's techniques but in my opinion fitted well within his codes of practice. I started by asking Rose her favourite fruit; she replied, 'Pineapple, cut into lovely juicy slices.'

I was surprised. I had her down as a more prosaic banana eater, not one to stray into the exotica of the pineapple – a fruit that I would classify as a special-occasion purchase. I explained that when she heard any of the following words she would think of and say pineapple, taking her to a place where her rage would disintegrate in the face of her favourite tropical fruit. I listed the main level-one swear words and threw in a few of my favourite but lesser used level-two insults, such as knob-cheese and wazzock. Once the list was complete, I snapped my fingers.

'You are now conscious, free of your linguistic burden, ready to take on the world.'

Rose's eyes blinked open, gaining focus, and she asked, 'What the pineapple happened there? It was pineapple weird. Why am I pineapple saying pineapple?'

I hadn't thought through the humorous consequences of my approach.

Nancy was not satisfied with my efforts and halted her weeding to tell me in no uncertain terms that it was, 'Tantamount to psychological abuse. Can you please put this right at once?'

While I had to agree that things hadn't gone to plan, I felt that labelling a bit of good-natured hypnotherapy gone wrong as abuse was an exaggeration.

Rose backed her up. 'For pineapple's sake, sort this pineapple well out!'

I thought it best that we saw how things played out over the next twenty-four hours, but with mounting pressure from Rose and Nancy, I was forced into reversing my work.

Once hypnotised again, I explained to Rose that swearing was a vital part of her personality, providing an outlet for her frustrations and helping her express her emotions when appropriate. The unfortunate by-product of the reversed hypnotic process was that I had to banish the word pineapple from her vocabulary. Its use was too risky, and so I decided that from now on she would describe it as the sweet fruit that dare not speak its name. I brought her back into consciousness and it was as if none of this awful episode had occurred. I made a note to get in touch with King Aziz and give some feedback on the pros and cons of his methods. He seems like a nice enough chap, but with the power he was wielding comes great responsibility.

Nancy requested that she take control of interview preparations from now on. It had been the moment I had been waiting for. Nancy was finally prepared to commit to the revolutionary process and put her skills to good use. After years of playing it safe, she was stepping foot into the land of the mavericks, the iconoclasts, the game-changers. I was flattered by her support, and, while not voiced, I could see that she saw me as a beacon of hope in troubled times. She wanted to surf in the wake of my wave and I was happy to oblige. We were two halves of a dynamic team, the heartbeat of Team Barry, not wishing to diminish the efforts of the other members. Comrades, we all have equal value in the struggle.

I wished Nancy and Rose good luck and stated that, 'If you stay true to my core beliefs and stick to the moral code as defined in the Seven Commandments, you will be sure to succeed. I have provided you the framework; now use it to guide you to victory.'

Their lack of response showed their implicit understanding and faith in my teachings. As a confident delegator and firm believer in gender equality, I was happy to leave them to their own devices, freeing up myself and Fairness Man to operate as an effective lone force.

It was time for Sophie and Nathan to return to the fulcrum of filth, elitism and inequality better known as London. I could see they were both empowered and energised from the weekend's events. I gave them maximum respect for being successful contestants in *Homeless House Invasion*, having not only built up a rapport with Rose but also being central in her efforts to enter employment. They had also been invaluable in imparting and activating their social media skills.

They had fallen in love with Fairness Man (I wish the same could be said of other members of Team Barry) and were happy to provide remote support to his content production and amplification. He had planted a seed of change that had sprouted and grown in their neural pathways, finding space between high-intensity workouts and filtered images of yoga pants. They had been present as the forces of change had collided, and their lives would never be the same again. As they discussed whether to stop off for a Nando's on the way home, I could tell it was in the context of a forever-altered perspective on society, community and individual freedoms. Bless you, my children, for you are the future; be free to enjoy the fast-food outlets of your choice, without compromising your values.

MONDAY APRIL 5ᵀᴴ

The day of reckoning had come. Fresh from the quiet reflection of the Sabbath, Team Barry was ready to scale Monday mountain. Monday: the beginning, the trough, the pit from which we must rise once more, comrades. Fairness Man had promised Abdul that today was the day that he would stare into the eyes of the Chief Environmental Officer and divert The Golden Tandoori away from the iceberg of oblivion and into the seas of salvation, where fish would nibble on left over samosas and turtles would dine out on chicken tikka masala.

I opened the drawer on my bedside table and pulled out the small framed picture of Lenny. Alas, it wasn't signed, but as hard as I tried, I couldn't find such an artefact. No surprises that the American techno-imperialist corporate machine eBay didn't stock authentic socialist memorabilia. In a moment of weakness, comrades, I succumbed to the modern-day ill of convenience and affordable pricing and clicked buy.

I looked into Lenny's steely eyes and requested guidance, but there was silence. His spirit was at rest. Either that or he was telling me it was time to stop leaning on him in times of need and make my own decisions. He was right, of course, but I was a bit deflated that he didn't want to input into the day's plans.

Nancy was already up and, having finished her breakfast, was concentrating on making sure Rose looked her best for the interview. She was blowdrying Rose's curly locks to give them extra bounce and volume. Rose's skin had taken on more colour after a couple of days at Barry Towers. The combination of good home cooking, a comfortable camp bed and an emotional support structure were already benefitting her health. I hadn't been monitoring the drinks cabinet, but while her tolerance levels were high, I sensed that her daily alcohol units were on the decline. If she landed the job at the bakers, I was hoping that this would be the fillip that would lead her down the path to a future free of the grip of liquor. I did need to attend to her wider housing and rehabilitative requirements, but for today I had to prioritise the joy of the peshwari naan dipped into madras sauce over the complex needs of a previously homeless and currently addicted citizen.

These are the difficult decisions that leaders such as myself have to make. I had to weigh up the cumulative value of The Golden Tandoori for hundreds of loyal customers versus the plight of one person. Thankfully, through the baseline of empowerment that I had fertilised, Rose had grasped the nettle of her cooking excellence and was set to grow spiritually, philosophically and economically in a way the curry-munching masses could only dream of, despite lacking the imagination to dream of anything beyond house extensions, holiday homes and the need to manage their cholesterol levels.

I had a feeling of nervous excitement that sent me back to May 8th, 1987, last day of the season in League Division Four. Alone in my room in the multiple-occupancy house, a young man with ambition, stepping onto the first rung of housing department administrative tasks and responsibilities. I sat on my bed listening to the radio and stared at my treasured Level 42 poster, as Southend secured promotion to Division Three. As a single tear of joy trickled down my cheek, I reached for a can of celebratory pilsner and looked into the white heat of the future. Fairness Man was free from the travails of footballing support. He was not weighed down by tribal conventions and was all the better for it. He'd scythe through the red tape clogging up the arteries of Surrey County Council and resuscitate its weary heart.

Nancy was making the finishing touches to Rose's makeup and doing her best to calm her nerves. Bobby, the traitor, was by Rose's side and providing further moral support. Rose was dressed in one of Nancy's suit jacket and skirt combos, and while it was a little on the large side for her emaciated frame, it gave her the air of a newsreader on regional TV. Her request for a 'stiff fucking vodka' had been turned down and Nancy had instead made her a nice cup of camomile tea. I wished them well and went upstairs to begin the necessary transformation.

As I looked at the cape, mask and neckerchief laid out on the bedroom floor, I could see them vibrate with energy.

These symbolic accoutrements had taken on a life of their own. I would write to Fancy That Fancy Dress of Newcastle upon Tyne and thank them for their role in creating something earth-shatteringly good. They were accidental heroes, but heroes nonetheless, worthy of an honour in my New Year's List.

Fairness Man's costume was on, with a minor adjustment. As he knew that he would need to operate at the top of his game to navigate Surrey County Council's corridors of power, he switched from his normal choice of jeans to some grey jogging bottoms. Their loose-fit cotton would provide that extra degree of comfort that was required when the finest margins were the difference between success and failure. He was normally opposed to performance-enhancing drugs, but as the twinging hip was still in play, he made a beeline to the bathroom and double-dropped some ibuprofen. He wanted to leave unseen, but the ever-alert Nancy caught him sneaking out. 'Oh, George, not again, please don't.'

But as much as she pleaded, he had to go.

'One day you will understand, my love. This is destiny, and nothing can stop its burgeoning web of wonderment.'

The Raleigh, untethered from the trailer, sped away from Barry Towers with a sense of dignity and purpose rarely seen this century. Fairness Man was sad that he couldn't be physically present at the interview, but when the moment came, at 9:00am to be precise, he would use his spiritual powers to guide Rose through the vocational interrogation. As he got into his rhythm, pedals turning, fields passing, the steady stream of morning commuter traffic was reluctantly off for another week of work, their dreams smothered by the leaden sky. He would cycle for them and their inconsequential lives. He would do all he could to fill them with meaning and at the very least enable the simple pleasure of a brown bag full of authentically prepared Indian dishes, watered down and adapted through Anglo-colonial influences.

Lost in an aerobic-induced meditation, he had lost track of time, and when he glanced at his Casio digital timepiece he saw it was 9:15. Rose had been flying solo, horns locked with Sandra Smythe in a bout of baked goods-related discourse. He was hoping Team Barry's hard work was paying off. To help give her an extra competitive advantage in the interview, he unleashed a grenade of religious vision. He pictured a yellow, green and white marzipan dove with a little white halo, gliding through Burhampton Bakers, before nestling on Sandra's shoulder and gently whispering, 'Give her the job, give her the job, give her the job'. Sandra looked to the dove, smiled, nodded, picked it up, bit its head off and cackled like the Wicked Witch of the West before melting into a puddle of sugary water, lapped up by dear Bobby, who scampered off, leaving Rose to build an empire based on her world-famous cakes. He knew that if Rose felt the emotional essence of this allegory, she would succeed.

Fairness Man cycled into Weyford, and as he took in the sights, he reminisced on adventures past and pushed back a wave of melancholy as he watched its damned residents complicit in their own downfall. An army of ants, ceaseless in their feeding of the capitalist machine, bereft of value and self-worth. Their day of enlightenment would come, but due to limited resources and the herculean effort needed to shift the direction of their tanker of ill-informed inertia, they would be near the back of the queue.

171

He parked up his bike outside the foreboding brutalist facade of Surrey County Council offices, Leighton Road, Weyford. I wish I had briefed Fairness Man on council culture and given him some tips on how to play the local government game, but I accepted he would have ignored them anyway. He walked with an assured gait as he scaled the concrete steps up to some revolving doors and through to the atrium. To his left lay the reception and ahead a security guard, keeping eye over two silver turnstiles. As the council workers arrived for a day's hopeless toil, they dabbed their security lanyards on a sensor by the turnstiles and carried on their way. The security guard was eyeballing Fairness Man and he knew he would need to find a loophole within the security protocol to gain entry.

He walked to the reception desk, and the receptionist, hair dyed blonde and with a liberal dose of fake tan, said, 'Oh, I like your costume. Are you raising money for charity? Prostate cancer, is it?'

He explained that while his presence on this important day was charitable in nature, what he would like was a meeting with the Chief Environmental Officer. The receptionist politely refused his request, as an appointment would need to be arranged in advance. Frustrated by the formal restrictions of civic bureaucracy, he used his evolving skills for improv performance and fell to the floor, gripping his chest and making a series of loud, agonising groans. Yes, an elite athlete like Fairness Man can have a cardiac episode, even if it's of the ersatz variety.

As he writhed on the floor gasping for air, he feebly pronounced, 'I think I'm g-g-g-going to d-d-die.'

The security guard – who I imagine had high morals, strong work ethic and, having spent time in the army during the Troubles, was well experienced in crisis situations – came to Fairness Man's assistance. The security guard bore down on him and started to administer heart-resuscitation techniques. As his hands pushed down on his chest, Fairness Man felt queasy and regurgitated some of his morning's breakfast, which he swallowed back down in time for the security guard to start giving mouth to mouth. Fairness Man took his opportunity and raised his right knee hard and fast into the security guard's testicles. This stopped his first-aid endeavours in their tracks and allowed Fairness Man to roll him over, leaving him prostrate and the turnstile unguarded. Fairness Man did not take pleasure in administering pain, but when it was vital to his progress he sanctioned its use, with the caveat that he caused no lasting damage. The receptionist, concerned for the security guard's wellbeing, came from around her desk to see to him. 'Johnny, are you OK, my dear?'

Fairness Man was able to vault – well, more like step over – the unsupervised silver turnstiles and gain access to Surrey County Council, the enemy of progress. By the lifts was a sign which listed that the Environmental Planning Department was on the seventh floor. He was normally a take-the-stairs kind of guy, grabbing the chance to push the limits of his cardiovascular ability, but he also enjoyed the engineering efficiency of the elevator, which he opted for after a quick cost-benefit analysis.

Stepping out on to the seventh floor, he entered an open-plan office. Desks and computer screens were arranged in conforming, unimaginative rows. The staff exchanged the age-old pleasantries, uttered without thought, with ears unreceptive to what people had got up to at the weekend, nodding, smiling, delaying the inauguration of another working week. At the far end was a glass-walled corner office, visible for transparency, sealed for secrecy: a manifestation of the hypocrisy that permeated every inch of the building. The desire to be open while needing to retain control, defend privilege and stifle progression. Oh, how I had suffered, drawn through the cogs of Basildon Council and spat out in a discombobulated heap. Only to rise again, a man of dignity, ready to engender a grassroots movement, comrades, where micro-organisations bonded with a shared belief and appreciation for administrative innovation, unleashing a tidal wave of reform. Yes, Fairness Man is their poster boy, but let's not forget the true heroes up and down the country (albeit only realistically being able to reach about 3–7% of his revolutionary prowess), signing up for the great fight. Ladies and gentlemen, we salute you.

Heads turned and there was a flurry of nervous tittering as he headed in the direction of the corner office. Rejected by the reception meeting arrangement protocol, he was going to break through the glass ceiling of council hierarchy and go straight to the source of power. The big cheeses, the decision-makers, the high rollers of the seventh-floor Mafioso. On the door to the office, the name and title of its inhabitant was displayed in a functional black font with a gold background. It read Mrs Amanda Hetherington, Chief Environmental Officer. Mrs Amanda Hetherington was sat behind her desk holding forth with two underlings, with sensible haircuts and sensible shoes, nodding in agreement every few seconds. Mrs Amanda Hetherington had perfectly groomed shoulder-length hair, jet-black with a smattering of grey. She had a sharp jawline and a Roman nose that gave her an air of dignified authority. She looked like a woman who demanded respect but paid it back with fair treatment and a generous Christmas bash for her team's hard work. Unfortunately, I had had to make do with John Moffat, a career-climbing vampire, sucking the blood from the pool of talent he had at his disposal.

Seeing that Mrs Amanda Hetherington needed to be treated with the reverence that she deserved, Fairness Man gave a courteous rap on the glass door before flinging it open and announcing his presence. While the Chief Environmental Officer was equipped in dealing with the unpredictable events of complex environmental policy, Fairness Man's presence threw her off her oft-chartered course of efficient delivery in meeting pre-set KPIs and departmental business targets. 'Is this some sort of practical joke? If so, it isn't funny. Can you leave immediately? Can't you see we are busy with important business?'

'Mrs Hetherington, if I may call you that, this is far from a joke. I have my own important business, which I lay before you to be inspected. The most important business that the parish of Burhampton has faced since reaching the Surrey County Bowls Championship in 1986. An event that preceded my involvement in the area but, needless to say, ended in tears that fell into the cauldron of discontent that has manifested into a cancerous ideology that fears cultural diversity and persecutes difference.'

He jumped onto Mrs Amanda Hetherington's desk and, with a fixed stare, started an improvised disco version of the star jump, which incorporated John Travolta's famous diagonal finger pointing to great effect. Mrs Hetherington usually dealt with employee misconduct with a formal process of verbal warnings, escalating in several clear steps to dismissal. She was less sure how to deal with Fairness Man in full flight, a force of energy that was nigh on impossible to tame. 'Get down at once or I'll call security.'

He turned in the air, landing to the side of the desk, and continued his routine, using different moves to represent his favourite curry items. He juddered his body to portray the heat of the vindaloo, he swayed his arms as a tribute to the aromatic enchantment of basmati and executed a forward roll that any six-year-old would be proud of: the embodiment of the culinary appetizer of the gods, the onion bhaji.

Mrs Hetherington and her minions looked on in wonder. His performance had hurtled through their compartmentalised brains and opened them up to a new world of self-expression.

'Yes, Mrs Hetherington, you have the future of curry at your fingertips. The Golden Tandoori, Burhampton, established 1995, average TripAdvisor rating of 4.5 stars, is under threat of closure and you decide its future.'

Mrs Amanda Hetherington looked down her prominent nose at Fairness Man and thanked him for his interesting performance. 'I cannot fault your passion, but I need to get on with my work. Sue, Jonathan, can you please check the progress of the case he refers to and then escort him out of the building. Good day, sir.'

Fairness Man is not one to take kindly to being fobbed off. I know how he feels having my requests, observations and departmental strategic recommendations repeatedly ignored by John Moffat. To be fobbed off is to be dehumanised, a living being whose voice is shut off and shut down. He was not another servile toad, ready to bow down in the face of the might of the Surrey County Council Employee Code of Conduct, but a sentient being, endowed with religious zest and political gusto. Using his sentience wisely, and being well aware that modern-day battles were fought in the cloud and not on the field, he grabbed Mrs Amanda Hetherington's laptop and made a run for it. He had the digital mothership of environmental decision-making in his hands, and he would not waste the opportunity to hack into the necessary database or administrative system to alter the course of history.

The ibuprofen was washing through Fairness Man's bloodstream, aiding a running speed that belied his years, outpacing Mrs Amanda Hetherington and her minions as they snaked through the desks to the lifts. Mrs Amanda Hetherington had dispatched with her high heels and held them in hand, ready to assail our hero. With no lifts available, he headed for the stairwell and made it down to the sixth-floor lift area, where he took cover in the men's toilets. The cubicles had floor-to-ceiling wooden doors, providing an excellent hiding place, not allowing entrance or infiltration from any angle. He thanked the person who designed the cubicle for their foresight in providing not only the acoustic privacy, which makes public defecation less off an auditory minefield for both the giver and receiver of unwelcome farts, squeaks and plops, but a cocoon for a high-level cyber assault.

He flipped open the laptop and was faced with an unfinished email with the subject 'Staff holiday allocation' to be sent to All Environment Staff. Mrs Amanda Hetherington and the minions had taken little time to track him down and were hammering on the door. 'Get out now or I'll call the police.'

He informed them that he was on good terms with members of Surrey Police Force, most notably Police Sergeant Button, and they would, he hoped, back him up in his fully lawful actions.

'But you have stolen council property, Mr whatever-your-name-is. Give it back now, and we will take this no further.'

Fairness Man knew that as it was council property, then it was de facto public property. He was not to be brow-beaten, as he heard the rap of metal heal on the wooden cubicle door.

'Please leave me in peace to hack your systems, Mrs Hetherington.'

She told him that, 'We have you surrounded, and we will be phoning the police immediately, so your time will soon be up.'

What she didn't know was that Fairness Man loved it when the odds were well stacked against him. When hanging from the precipice of desolation, he didn't worry about falling but instead imagined how wonderful it would be to master the art of flight, swooping up above the concerns of institutionalised bureaucrats. His eyes were drawn back to the email, where he saw the opportunity to drop a high-powered thought bomb into their inboxes.

Dear people,

I am writing on behalf of the spiritual subconscious of Mrs Amanda Hetherington. Beneath my tough exterior there is a caring soul fighting to get out. I had a challenging childhood, and it has led to some personality flaws that you are probably aware of. My parents showed little care for my emotional development, prioritising academic achievement over all else. As a result, I am highly ambitious but lack the interpersonal skills of a more rounded individual, such as this masked chap I've just met. I think he goes by the name of Fairness Man, and if you search him online, you'll find lots of superb content, which is not only entertaining but informative. If only I could live up to the example he has set. To start making good for any sins I may have committed in the past, such as my overzealous biscuit consumption on some of my darker days, I should like to inform the department that our environmental planning decisions need to be taken through the lens of social justice and community cohesion.

It has come to my attention that The Golden Tandoori, Burhampton, is under review for infringements of environmental law, driven by an organisation with an abhorrent desire to stamp its Anglo-Saxon white supremacist ideals on all, and deny residents their rights to consume the best ethnic cuisine that the south-west corner of Surrey has ever seen. Whoever is overseeing this case, can you make sure that said curry house passes with flying colours and is able to carry on trading unhindered?

If anyone is passing through Burhampton, feel free to pay George Barry, at Barry Towers, Elm Lane, a visit. He is currently in political exile but is building a better world, where, my dear little administrative ant army, you will have the opportunity to cleanse yourself of the filth that has burrowed deep into your every pore and crevice after years of wallowing in the cesspit of council *life, worn down by the pernicious management structure and the anally retentive stationery ordering system. There will be a holistic workshop itinerary at your disposal, combining mindfulness, collectivism, behavioural bias acceptance and theological deconstruction, to create a shit-hot manual for personal transformation that layers into a radical recalibration of societal interactions. There is hope, comrades, seize the opportunity and shed the pupa of shame and emerge as a butterfly of belief.*

> *Peace out,*
> *Mrs Amanda Hetherington*

p.s. Hit me up if you would like to expand on any of the points raised above.

He hit send and felt a frisson of pleasure from inhabiting the mind of the Chief Environmental Officer and funnelling her power for the greater good. I think the technical term is identity fraud, but he had no doubt that, given time to reflect, Mrs Amanda Hetherington would be thanking him for penning an email that has helped her bridge the gap with an already disaffected workforce who were desperate for some new thinking to be injected into their predictable lives. As her high heels hammered against the toilet door, he could tell she wasn't in a reflective mood at present. 'Get out of there and give me my laptop at once, for Christ's sake.'

Fairness Man remained silent as he planned his escape. He reached out to Ganesha, but the spiritual signal strength was muted by the thick wood of the cubicle door, and he could only make out an incomprehensible whisper. He listened again and made out what he thought was, 'Shed your skin, then let him in.' He was irked that Ganesha had to be so bloody obtuse, but they were a product of a certain time and culture when straight-talking was not in vogue.

He could feel his bowels churn, and he thought it only right to make use of the lavatorial throne on which he sat. He also found that his mental abilities were enhanced during the process of expurgating bodily waste, so with expedience, he got down to the job at hand. With the police on their way, he added haste to his normal relaxed pace when it came to the matters of the water closet. The excrement flowed out and, feeling lighter in mind and body, it came to him. 'Shed your skin, then let him in.' Yes, it was time for Fairness Man to shed his skin and let me into the arena in which I was borne to excel, i.e. local government administration. He said goodbye, thanking all those who had passed through this cubicle before and enjoyed its peaceful solitude. He was at one with their suffering and the spiritual power of a good poo.

I sat and waited for the stench to subside and grieved his absence. Like an annoying older brother who stole your sweets, pretended you didn't exist and ridiculed your devotion to ELO's earlier canon, he was missed when he was gone. I opened the door and held out the laptop as a peace offering.

'Thank God for that. You've taken off that silly costume and come to your senses,' said Mrs Amanda Hetherington, taking back the computer and cradling it to her chest, an electronic baby returned to the suckling of her mother.

I told her that, 'Fairness Man's unconventional but

effective results driven work is done, and you are free to continue going about your day.'

'That may be so, but you can save your energy and explain this to the police. I've got a very important 10:30, so must be on my way,' she said, turning about face and leaving with minion one and two in tow, leaving me alone with a security guard, who, I ascertained from his lanyard, was Simon Eze and, from his accent, he hailed from Africa.

Broad-shouldered, standing to attention, he asked me to, 'Stay with me, Sir, until the police officers arrive.'

I couldn't argue with a man who took to his task with dignity and politeness, qualities that hark back to a better day when respect for fellow human beings was paramount.

We both agreed it would be preferable that we stood outside of the men's toilets to respect the privacy of people's morning ablutions. We moved out to the lift area, and, with time to spare, I explained the rationale behind Fairness Man's actions and how he had used Mrs Amanda Hetherington's laptop for the purpose of vital communications, which would redress the inherent bias that is undermining the diversity of British society.

Simon Eze was unequivocal in his response. 'Sir, theft is sin. It is plainly stated in the Bible. I'm sorry, but you are guilty, and I can't condone your behaviour.'

I continued by detailing how Fairness Man had moved the Bible forward and reframed its basic tenets, while retaining the commandment framework. I stated that theft was still definitely a religious no-no, but the temporary requisition of council property for the greater social good was permissible. I could see from his curious expression that he was digging the vibes of this new ethos but was resisting the urge to sign up on the dotted line of a contract for political and spiritual realignment. I tried to seal the deal by making him an honorary disciple. I explained that myself and Rolly were privileged white men, and while we were happy to guide and dictate a better way of living that applies to all minority groups, it would be great to have someone of colour on board (I would need to open a correspondence with Lucy from Portsmouth and check her ethnic makeup, as we may have the diversity box already ticked). I said that he would be a vital ethnic sounding board. Comrades, this direct and honest approach did not work as expected.

Rather than being grateful for the generous opportunity I had offered, Simon Eze was most put out and, I would go as far as saying, irked. 'Sir, I will not be your token black man. I do not want to be a sounding board. I have my own beliefs and culture; all I ask is for you to respect them.'

We had reached an ideological impasse. I was tempted to bridge the divide by referring to my appreciation of the commercial end of reggae, in particular Maxi Priest, but decided that the time wasn't right. While Fairness Man had been successful in connecting with a younger profile, there was a diversity issue that would have to be addressed. Here's where, once again, I would need the help from the metropolitan branch of Team Barry, namely Sophie and Nathan. While I was on first-name terms with Abdul, of The Golden Tandoori, and Mehmet, proprietor of Burhampton Newsagents, who I've had many a brief chat regarding the state of the nation and the latest sporting events, as a man of humility and on a quest for constant self-improvement, I knew there was work to be done.

Fresh from Fairness Man's recent successful sparring

match with Larton Police, I felt no concern for the imminent arrival of the local law enforcement. I looked out of the windows in the lift area as I gazed down on my geographic nemesis, Weyford, and out into the distance towards Burhampton. From up high I could imagine a different world, reminiscent of Trumpton, where the bell rang for the end of the working day and the obedient citizens filed out ready for some wholesome leisure time with family and friends. If I thought hard enough, I could see a community that supported each other in the hard times and shared in celebration of the good times. If I could make change here, I could make it anywhere.

The utopian spell was broken when Simon Eze tapped me on my shoulder and let me know that the police had arrived. The woman and man who emerged from the lift, wearing wholly unnecessary high-vis jackets for daytime operations – an ostentatious signal that they were so bloody important that they warranted everyone's attention. The female police officer was short and sturdy, with dark brown hair pulled back in a tight bun, and the male police officer gangly, with a reptilian face and a pair of greasy blond curtains that were welded to his forehead. They looked barely old enough to order a pint and more suited to crowd control at a toddler's party than dealing with a maverick of my stature, a man whose alternative identity had already made a strong personal connection with Larton Police's generalissimo.

Simon Eze gave a rundown of my misconduct: stating that I had committed physical harm on a member of security staff, forced entry into the building, while then invading the meeting space of a senior member of staff before stealing her laptop. The police lapped up this literal description of events and there was no point attempting to get them to think otherwise. If only Police Sergeant Button was present, we could short-circuit this needless protocol that was wasting time and diverting attention away from serious crime. My patience was running low, and I needed to take matters back in hand. There were people's lives who depended on me and would suffer if I was detained. I was needed, and drastic situations demand drastic solutions. To my benefit, I had watched countless police dramas and had built up an encyclopaedic knowledge of criminal tactics. I said that I would be ready to go to the police station once I had been to the toilet, as I feared I may soil myself in transit due to incontinence brought on by stress and my nervous disposition. The policing duo took the bait, and through subtle shifts in my demeanour, using my now-proficient improv skills, I inhabited the body of a lesser able man.

As I limped to the door, hunch-backed, they asked me to, 'Hurry up, we haven't got all day.'

I'm sure they've got time to check Facebook whilst people's homes are broken into, cars stolen and society slowly plunges into chaos, so have the decency to let an old and broken man have the chance to empty his faulty bowels at his own pace, you animals. I'd read a lot about police brutality, but I was now experiencing it first-hand. When the chance arises, I'll shoot the breeze with Police Sergeant Button, or the Buttster to mates, and work out how we can integrate the relevant models of empathetic mindfulness into a wider programme of communications training for the rank and file.

Simon Eze stood guard outside my cubicle of choice,

second from the left. I already felt a connection to the space and was pleased to have made such a fast return. I went through the facade of my faux shit by dropping my trousers and sitting on the porcelain throne. I felt a sense of disappointment that I was unable to take part in the real act. Like a pop star lip-synching to his fans, I felt like a fraud, acting out a treasured bodily procedure, defaming its rightful place in the cycle of life. On the lavatory we are all equal, comrades. As the Queen famously said, 'Dear servants, one's shit doth smell, and you'd better give it five minutes before you go in there.'

While I was ready to step forward and be questioned on the trumped-up charges of this tin-pot operation, Fairness Man had plans of his own. He took over my hands and, rifling under my sweatshirt, pulled out his costume. He took a deep breath to summon the strength of an ox, the speed of a puma and the navigational awareness of a homing pigeon needed to override Ganesha's commands. He sprung open the door and cast a glance over himself in the mirror. With a few days of facial hair growth, he had developed a rugged look that harked back to Clint in his golden years, walking the Spanish plains tight-lipped and fast-triggered, ready to shoot Lee Van Cleef's hat through the dust, as the clock ticked down to the moment of reckoning.

Simon Eze attempted to grab Fairness Man, but with a side shimmy he dodged the hands of authority and made his way out of the toilets. Back in the lift area, he was faced with PC Tight Bun and PC Curtains, who by his calculations had the potential to match both his speed and strength, i.e. the ox, and the puma but not the homing abilities, i.e. the pigeon. He fluttered the wings of his cape and cooed as the police approached, ready to entrap the great man. He turned and ran to the stairwell, and, remembering childhood days, sliding down Aunt Beryl's bannisters, he mounted the hand rail and descended to floor five, the residence of the housing department. As he made his way out of the stairwell into the lift area, he darted into a cleaning cupboard. PC Curtains and PC Tight Bun were hot on his heels, rapped on the cupboard door and asked him to step out. Gracious in defeat, he walked out of the cupboard and blessed the young officers, wishing them redemption and a fruitful reincarnation, where, if lucky, they would re-emerge further up the law enforcement food chain. PC Curtains, ignorance personified, snapped a handcuff shut on Fairness Man's wrist and locked the other cuff to himself.

'Your time's up, sonny, you're nicked,' he said with a smile. To be honest, that must be the best bit of his job, and I couldn't begrudge him his moment of happiness.

They led him out of the building to the parked police car, metres away from the Raleigh – an ancient and dignified form of transportation compared to the gas-guzzling choice of the modern crime fighter. While the pair basked in the glory of snaring a local and international icon of change, their hubris was their undoing. The keys to the handcuffs hung from PC Curtains' hip on a large silver carabiner. As the doors opened to the passenger seat, Fairness Man swiped the keys with his spare hand and undid his cuff, throwing the keys into a nearby hedge.

'They don't teach you these advanced escape methods at police school, do they?' he said, laughing at their incompetence.

He ran to the Raleigh and cycled off with PC Tight Bun pulling his cape, causing a moment of asphyxiation, which he alleviated by undoing the knot that fixed it around his neck, sending her tumbling to the tarmac. As he cycled down a path that led around the back of the council HQ, he mourned the passing of his cloak of invincibility.

The path led down to a river: a quiet retreat where a couple of men were sat fishing and dog walkers idled away a spare hour with their companions. In the water was a moored rowing boat named *Bertha*, unattended, which attracted the perceptive eye of Fairness Man. He is not a man of maritime distinction, preferring the dependable resistance of foot on terra firma. This aversion to the bobbing wave and the riparian ripple was about to change. With PC Curtains and PC Tight Bun breathing down his neck, projecting the stench of vending-machine coffee and cheese and onion crisps, he had no choice but to untie *Bertha*, leap into the wooden vessel and set sail with the assistance of an outboard motor fixed to its rear.

It soon became clear that the boat belonged to one of the fishermen, who had noticed it had been requisitioned and was drifting at four to five miles an hour, or the equivalent knots, downstream.

The fisherman set off in pursuit down the riverside path a few metres behind the police, who were attempting to halt Fairness Man in his progress by asking that he, 'Please disembark, disembark at once, you're making a big mistake, resisting arrest is a crime, we don't want to have to get our police uniforms wet now, do we?'

The fisherman pleaded, 'Stop, thief, don't go off with my lovely *Bertha*. She's always been there for me: strong, silent, unjudging and supportive, through good times and bad.'

Fairness Man was no cad. He felt remorse when bumping heads with the evil twins of selfish intent and reckless individuality. He could not strip *Bertha* away from this dear fellow, who, while being a Weyford resident, didn't emanate the usual glow of status-obsessed contempt. Through the humble pastime of angling, he'd learnt the value of patience, a respect for nature and opened himself to the possibility of a pescatarian diet. He also realised that *Bertha* didn't have the required speed to outstrip his pursuers and so in an act of charity and expedience, he switched off the motor and dived overboard.

In a few well-applied breaststrokes, he was at the opposite riverbank, where, with the help of a clump of overgrown grass, he pulled himself up and out of the water. If only Nancy could see Fairness Man in all his brilliance: combining physical agility and rapid intelligence to reach the zenith of human capability. Will she ever know him for who he really is?

He looked back over to the opposite bank and stared into the indecisive eyes of the inexperienced bobbies. It is these split-second prevarications that separate the sheep from the able shepherd, shepherdess or sheep-management specialist. Traversing watery expanses was not part of modern police training, and while they dithered, Fairness Man made his way through a gap in a fence that led onto a school playing field, where a group of children were taking part in a game of hockey. It was not a sport in which he had any prior knowledge, but he was pleased to see the next generation away from the lure of the screen and enjoying the satisfaction of foot on grass and stick on ball.

The games master was bellowing commands at his pupils, admonishing any mistake and doing his best to destroy any seeds of confidence. He would do his level best to ensure they didn't eclipse his personal achievement of representing Surrey for three consecutive seasons, the last of which he was awarded captaincy. Every day he would walk past his trophy cabinet and regret that ankle injury that halted his trajectory to the national team and the chance of Olympic glory.

As Fairness Man ran along the touchline towards the school building, he complimented the children on their hockey craft and clarified that his trespassing was a necessary requirement in evading incarceration and the detrimental effects on society that would materialise as a result. The children stopped playing and laughed as he made his way past. He had the innate ability to connect with the younger generations, their minds open to change and ready to embrace humour as a welcome antidote to a curriculum that was preparing them for a life of turgid obedience.

'Please leave the premises before I call the police!' shouted the games master. But he would have been pleased to see that he had no need to take this course of action, as through the fence appeared the drenched officers.

Fairness Man had earned himself the valuable seconds needed to make his way around the front of the school, go onto the adjoining main road and hide himself from PC Tight Bun and PC Curtains in a glass bottle recycling bin. Nestled amongst the empty bottles, breathing in the stale stench of booze, he waited. He felt it was an apt hiding place, sizable enough to house his well-proportioned frame on this occasion while also reflecting his green beliefs. He peered through the brush-rimmed recycling slot and saw no sign of the hapless policing duo. They must be on their way back to the station, ready to tell of their incompetence. He felt sorry that they had encountered a power far beyond their rank. They would recover from the humiliation and rebuild their careers, but for now they were unwitting martyrs to the cause.

He clambered out of the bin, a little woozy from its vapours. He was now officially on the run. He craved the input from his collaborative partners, who he'd come to rely on for their wisdom, good humour and acumen, but try as he might to conjure their presence, they were nowhere to be seen.

A swift return to Burhampton was in order, but with the Raleigh abandoned and the magic powers of ibuprofen ebbing, he decided to throw himself into the arms of the benevolent but unreliable arms of South West Surrey's public transport provision. While buses met his utilitarian, sustainable credo, the stopping protocol jarred with the restless need for continual progress.

After a short wait at a conveniently placed request stop, he stepped foot on the number 24 bus. I had great affection for the route that traversed the spine of South West Surrey, linking Weyford to Burhampton and beyond. From the top deck – right-hand side when leaving Burhampton and left-hand side on your return – there was an unrestricted view of the countryside, with the occasional interruption from a retail outlet, petrol station or housing enclave. Fairness Man followed suit and walked up to the top deck and went to the rear, the territory favoured by teenagers with a penchant for anti-social behaviour.

As he sat, forced into temporary inactivity, he worried that he was ahead of his time, another pioneer only to be respected once he was dead. He didn't want to be another Van Gogh, selling his art just to survive, slowly ground into misery before deciding to fell a fully functioning ear, leaving himself hideously disfigured, an outcast, who in time would be considered a colossus standing at the epicentre of human achievement. Added to that, he was starting to crave a mid-morning snack and had neglected to pack provisions. As the bus headed out of town and past M&S, with its bountiful supply of pork pies and Percy Pigs, he let out a wistful sigh. His energy was depleted, but he'd have to do without, a brave warrior stalking the hinterland of hunger, sacrificing his love for premium snacks for the greater good. He hoped that Rose had been successful in overcoming her verbal inflictions during her interview, and there would be a celebratory slice of cake awaiting back at Barry Towers. A safe space for him and the team to rejoice away from the evil forces that stalked his every step.

He turned away from the window and to his right sat a young lad of no more than fourteen, who, seeing Fairness Man's mask, gave a nod of recognition. 'Nice get-up, mate. Proper funny, geezer.'

The voice of disaffected youth speaking loud and true. Fairness Man raised his fist ready for a bump, the less satisfying urban cousin to the handshake, but the youth was now occupied by his mobile screen, drawing him in and providing a place of comfort. He laughed as he watched a skateboarder fall off and smash his face on concrete. Desensitised from suffering, he sought solace in the visceral humour of pain.

Fairness Man had the hopes of a generation on his

shoulders. He would voice their concerns, giving them their rightful place on the world stage. They were annexed, like an intellectual Poland, ready to be subsumed by the fascist reign of angry old white men. Yes, you are right to point out that Fairness Man is a white man, with the occasional bouts of anger, but his inner peace and respect for the majority of the social ecosystem, with added pious positivity, meant he subverted the potential ills of his demographic, to create a model that represented myriad concerns.

Approaching Burhampton, his senses were heightened, when a police car overtook the bus, with its sirens blaring. He looked down and saw the unmistakable bald white head of Police Sergeant Button in the driver's seat. The big man had been brought back into play and he meant business. He was Clarice to Fairness Man's Hannibal Lecter. He was the one person who understood his unique psychological profile (it's important to note that he didn't harbour any desires to murder and eat his fellow humans). Two goliaths pitting themselves against each other to the bitter end.

Fairness Man descended the stairs of the number 24 bus at the stop opposite St Mary's Church. In his heart he knew it was his spiritual home and that Reverend Ormerod had outstayed his welcome, but due to time pressures, forced entry, eviction and the start of a period of spiritual squatting, supported by a pew-based barricade, were off today's menu. Reverend Ormerod, your idle life of empty words and afternoon tea will carry on for a while, but don't sit comfortably; the creeping claw of reformation is upon you.

He reached the high street with trepidation. In the distance he spotted Police Sergeant Button's car parked outside The Golden Tandoori, with a small crowd forming beside it. A parked police car was something of an event in Burhampton, which prided itself on one of the lowest crime rates in the county, according to its own residents and not based on any statistical evidence. There had been a recent spate of garden shed break-ins from someone who, according to sources on Burhampton Forum, appeared to have an obsession for trowels. The Spatchcocks had put this crime spree down as the inevitable consequence of Eastern Europeans being allowed to settle in the UK.

Fairness Man knew Buttmeister would be tormented, placed between the rock of dependable and reasonably priced Asian cuisine and the hard place of having to arrest one of the finest members of the human race to have ever stepped foot on the well-kept paving slabs of Burhampton High Street. He didn't want to second-guess what the criminal-vanquishing mastermind would do next. As he weighed up his options, he spotted a Ban Barry poster in the window of the newsagents. Rolly P's intelligence was verified and correct. Under a less-than-flattering photo, used without my permission, infringing both copyright and intellectual property law, and the 'Ban Barry' slogan, 'Don't interact with him. Don't serve him. Don't encourage him', was the sinister propaganda of the fascist Spatchcockian pen. Its vicious tone and horrendous bending of the truth bore the mark of Jeremy Simmonds.

> *'This man is a force of evil. His reckless support for undesirable members of society will drag us all down and have a potential downward impact on house prices of 2.5%. Not only does he support the repulsive odours that are allowed to pollute our air, he has brought a homeless*

waif into our parish. Please under no circumstances have any social or commercial interaction with this man. It is your civic duty to comply. Your actions will be observed and judged. Keep your eyes peeled and your doors firmly shut.'

Fairness Man empathised with my plight, but he was in desperate need of a Kit Kat Chunky. While he knew he should boycott this establishment in solidarity, he had to strike a balance. He is the master of tactical compromise: something I struggle with, with my unerring principles and utopian vision.

My acquaintance and good ethnic friend Mehmet was happy to serve him. 'They say I shouldn't serve you, George, but don't worry, I treat my customers with respect.'

While Fairness Man was annoyed to be lumped into my blanket retail ban, he was pleased to see the flagrant disregard for the Spatchcockian diktat. The resistance was forming. I knew I could rely on you, comrades. In every nook, cranny, corner, crevice, alley and side passage, we will stand up and take our rightful place at the altar of capitalist transaction, while questioning and contemplating a fairer system with, as of yet, not having a complete plan for its overhaul.

He bowed to Mehmet and thanked him for his kindness. He wanted to give him his blessing and offer a five-minute crash course of spiritual solace, but time was pressing, so he paid for his Kit Kat Chunky and said goodbye. He returned to the high street and saw Sergeant Button's car was heading away from The Golden Tandoori in his direction. He stood behind a lamp post, obscuring his entire face but little of his muscular frame, as the police car sped by, sirens blaring.

Fairness Man avoided the meandering shoppers that stood in his way and took to the road, breaking into a slow canter towards the curry house. As the shoppers looked on in awe as he sped past, he started humming the *Chariots of Fire* theme tune – a surefire winner when he needed to reach his athletic peak. As the epic chimes of Vangelis flowed out his mouth, into his ears and through his body, he imagined the soft sand beneath his feet, Team Barry cheering him on as he sprinted towards his destiny.

He stepped on the threshold to The Golden Tandoori, ready to inform Abdul of his quest. The curry-based caterer stood smiling. 'They've seen sense, George, there are no bloody environmental infringements, I can bloody well stay open.'

He passed Fairness Man the letter which he could see was dated two days prior. Fairness Man stood in shock. Not even he could have foreseen that his power could retrospectively impact on environmental planning decisions. He looked up to the ceiling, and looking down on him were Lenny, Ganesha and what looked like baby Jesus, all giving him a thumbs-up. Not only had he taken on their mantel but he had bettered it. As far as he was aware, none of this revered group could bend time at their whim. They waved to him as their images faded into the white aertex ceiling – an underrated building material that I have always been fond of but not to the point of wishing to apply it to the interior of Barry Towers. Fairness Man realised that we were at the dawn of a new era where his support team would have little part to play. Apart from the occasional cameo appearance, they would be hanging up their boots of their respective belief systems. With the believers of two major religions and one discredited political system to update, it would need a global PR push to cover nearly half of the world's population. With the well-crafted use of animated GIFs, I'm sure the job could be done at haste, but I was relieved that Jews, both progressive and orthodox, Muslims, Buddhists, Rastafarians and Sikhs were not included, as of yet.

He walked out of the curry house, head high, chest puffed and the impediment of an aching hip, which was crying out for rest, or at least another recommended dose of ibuprofen. The odd negative comment was thrown his way, but he took the words freak, nutter and leftie slag, and wore them as badges of honour, coming from the mouths of people whose minds were manipulated by playing on their fear and greed. From out of the sea of hate appeared the welcome face of Rolly P, who, as informant numero uno, told Fairness Man that, 'The police are waiting to get you – you mustn't go home.' Fairness Man had to reassure our timid friend that he needn't cower from authority any more. We were vindicated by the Environmental Planning Department and we would march on together to our fate.

Outside Barry Towers was the shiny vehicle of the Butt Man and beside it a braying crowd, with Jeremy Simmonds, Chinny Wilkinson, the Swine and Mr Cheese at the front. As Fairness Man approached, they chanted, 'Ban Barry, lock him up, ban Barry, lock him up' – primitive words from primitive people.

Comrades, they can lock me up, but they can't lock up our ideas. They had been set free and are floating into the front rooms, hostelries and smoking parlours of this fair isle. There was no suppressing their call for a better life.

Fairness Man stood, thumping his chest, and declared, 'I

have triumphed. The Golden Tandoori has been spared and this minute is preparing the beautiful pungent cuisine that span its ample menu. I have quashed your petty prejudice. Go home and spare me your repressed anger. In time you may rethink your views and values, and my colleague George Barry will be happy to sign you up to one of his many programmes for individual and societal betterment.' Deep down he knew they were beyond redemption, locked in their cell of illusory superiority.

The cold, sunken eyes of Jeremy Simmonds glared: a man not used to defeat but who would have to admit he had been outfought this time. Pushed out of his cosseted life surrounded by cronies, he had not fared well in a contest with Fairness Man's spiritual-political pugilism. Sorry, Jezza, but you and your boys have taken a right beating this time.

'I hope they lock you up and throw away the key,' Jeremy bellowed.

Victory was ours, and if we had to spend some time inside one of the nation's underfunded penal correction facilities, so be it.

Rolly acted as a helpful buffer between myself and the crowd as I approached Barry Towers.

He told them that, 'Fairness Man is a man of great fortitude, who has inspired me to face my weaknesses and start on the slow journey to overcome my neurosis and live a courageous life in his name. I am happy that through his hard work in maintaining the place of The Golden Tandoori within the limited but high-quality choice of catering outlets in the village, I can continue my ritual of a Saturday-night curry, a ritual also cherished by Mrs P' – or words to that effect.

I could see that the Swine, rubbing his belly in delight, was secretly pleased with this turn of events.

Inside Barry Towers, the King of the Butts was chatting with Nancy and Rose.

He got to his feet. 'I'm sorry, George, but I gave you a chance and you threw it in my face. I'm going to have to arrest you and this time you are going to pay your dues to society.'

Society was Fairness Man's master, and while every one of his actions was in its name, he would serve his time. A martyr whose followers will rise and continue the fight in his temporary absence.

Rose smiled. 'I did it, George, I only went and got the bloody job. I start tomorrow.'

Fairness Man was overjoyed that the wheels of change were finally turning. He congratulated Rose and voiced regret that he would miss her initial period of employment, but when he was free to walk the streets of Burhampton, with the proviso that the 'Ban Barry' campaign had subsided, he would be tasting her freshly baked delights on a daily basis. Rose confirmed that she would also be baking savoury pastries, including a pork and apple sausage roll, which he earmarked as his go-to afternoon snack.

He looked in awe at Nancy; she had unfathomable qualities that brought out the best in everyone. Without her strong, if sometimes critical, support, the revolution would have crumbled long ago. She rose to her feet and went and hugged him. I was pleased to see her animosity to Fairness Man was fading. Through mutual acceptance, a bond was forming – not in the biblical sense, as Fairness Man was not a man to step on my matrimonial shoes. Tears ran down her face. She would miss him when he was gone.

Fairness Man, from humble beginnings you have reached great heights. Flanked by dear Bobby, he ran out of the kitchen, locking the door behind, and headed to the woods. The chirp of the sparrow, the scamper of a nervous squirrel, the rustle of a playful hedgehog going about its daily routine. He felt a patch of earth and knelt. He took his mask and neckerchief off, and I dug into the earth with my bare hands to form a small hole. I placed the mask and neckerchief into the hole and covered them over with earth. Comrades, we were on our way.